…ether on a lonely … at Barrier Reef, …me of hide-and- …y both his parents and, having turned first to petty crime, is now into something much more dangerous. Lew, on the other hand, is indulged by doting parents, but he too faces a serious disadvantage of his own.

What could be in the mysterious box which Col keeps diving for in a desperate attempt to recover it from under the sea? And will the island, which Lew had felt was his own, ever be the same again? The conflict between these two very different characters is the basis of this truly gripping adventure story.

Allan Baillie was born in Scotland in 1943, but moved with his family to Australia when he was seven. On leaving school, he worked as a journalist and travelled extensively. He is now a full-time writer and is the author of five highly acclaimed novels for children. He is married with two children and lives in Sydney.

EAGLE ISLAND

ALLAN BAILLIE

PUFFIN BOOKS

PUFFIN BOOKS

Published by the Penguin Group
27 Wrights Lane, London W8 5TZ, England
Viking Penguin Inc., 40 West 23rd Street, New York, New York 10010, USA
Penguin Books Australia Ltd, Ringwood, Victoria, Australia
Penguin Books Canada Ltd, 2801 John Street, Markham, Ontario, Canada L3R 1B4
Penguin Books (NZ) Ltd, 182–190 Wairau Road, Auckland 10, New Zealand

Penguin Books Ltd, Registered Offices: Harmondsworth, Middlesex, England

First published in Australia by Thomas Nelson Australia 1987
First published in Great Britain by Blackie and Son Ltd 1987
Published in Puffin Books 1989
1 3 5 7 9 10 8 6 4 2

Baillie, Allan, 1943–
Eagle Island.

ISBN 0 14 034045 9.

I. Title.

A823'.3

Printed and bound in Great Britain by
Cox & Wyman Ltd, Reading
Filmset in Bembo

Contents

My thanks to the people of Airlie Beach and Shute Harbour, to the OD units of Proserpine and Chatwood and to Pat Murray for their tolerance and advice. And to Tim Nobes and Darren Webster for the best of Lew.

The research for *Eagle Island* was assisted by a Special Purpose Grant from the Australian Arts Council.

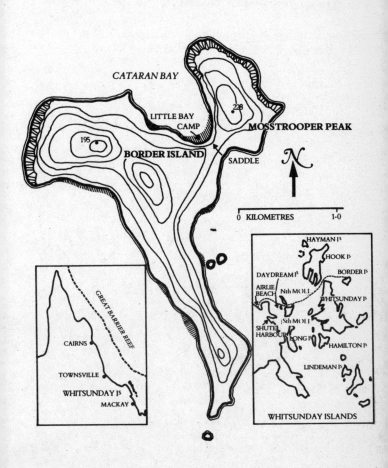

CATARAN BAY

LITTLE BAY
CAMP

228

MOSSTROOPER PEAK

195

BORDER ISLAND

SADDLE

N

0 KILOMETRES 1·0

GREAT BARRIER REEF

CAIRNS

TOWNSVILLE

WHITSUNDAY Iˢ

MACKAY

HAYMAN Iˢ

HOOK Iˢ

DAYDREAM Iˢ

BORDER Iˢ

AIRLIE
BEACH

Nth MOLL

WHITSUNDAY Iˢ

Sth MOLL

SHUTE
HARBOUR

LONG Iˢ

HAMILTON Iˢ

LINDEMAN Iˢ

WHITSUNDAY ISLANDS

1

The Clown

Col Starkey was looking for trouble.

He wasn't aware of this. He was simply hunched on
the cold metal of a gas cylinder watching the sky flame
over the Coral Sea, suffering from his bruised little toe
to his quietly throbbing head, and he hated the world.
He was not ready for today. He was not ready for this
week. Call back in a month.

Col shielded his eyes from the brightening sky and
jabbed a stick at a thin column of ants.

He had put up with a very bad night and today was
not going to be any better. He had run around a crowd
of tourists, feeding them, serving them drinks, laughing
at their lousy jokes, cleaning up after them, for tips a
kid wouldn't take as pocket money. And then one of
them went and called him a thief. Would have flattened
him, except for his rugby mates. Bunch of apes.

Col dropped pebbles on the ants.

He felt tired, bloated from all that food and drink
he'd taken on the run. His eyes were liked poached
eggs, and he probably looked as bad as he felt. Too
bad. He had not combed his long black hair, he was
still wearing yesterday's jeans and T-shirt and a bruise
was coming up on the side of his face where that tourist
had hit him. At least he still had the tourist's money.

Col rolled his big hands into fists and studied them carefully.

But that was yesterday. Today was going to be worse. There was only one thing that turned him off more than the tourists shuttling through Airlie Beach and that was Fat Theo. He was about as funny as a wild pig in a paddock, all the time snorting and throwing his weight about. And all day today Col was going to be working for Fat Theo on the Reef. Unless they were caught.

Col picked up another pebble and considered the red speedboat moored twenty metres away in Airlie Creek.

It would be sweet to heave a rock at Theo's stupid boat, but with the way his luck was running he would be seen. It would be more trouble than it was worth.

Anyway, where was Theo?

Col squirmed on the long gas cylinder under him and searched for a target for his pebble.

If Theo wanted him at Airlie Creek by sun-up then for sure he ought to be here himself.

Col stopped looking, and smiled.

A small catamaran was creeping toward the rocky mouth of the creek. It was moved by only a small jib, a faded handkerchief of a sail hanging almost dead from the mast, but a single brown boy was shifting about on the trampoline deck as if he was riding a squall.

Lew. Could only be Lew, Col thought. Nobody else makes sailing a comedy act.

Col threw the pebble at the incoming catamaran but missed and Lew didn't seem to notice the splash. He nosed the cat along the curve of stacked black boulders that protected the creek waters. Ignoring the jib, he picked up a small paddle from the deck and pushed himself past the speedboat.

Col bet with himself: three dollars he clowns about.

Lew turned the catamaran to the sand, released the jib and stood up. He replaced the paddle on the deck as the bow slid against the beach. Then he stepped to the edge of the deck.

Col was disappointed.

Then Lew leapt into the air and clapped his hands, as if a band had begun to play. He landed on the sand with both legs bent, straightened and shuffled toward the stone steps, waving an imaginary hat and twirling an imaginary cane. He danced half way up the steps, down again, up to the top and stopped with a flourish.

'Three dollars,' Col muttered.

Lew smiled uncertainly when he saw Col was watching him, then dropped the smile when it was not returned. He walked quickly toward the road behind Col.

''Allo mate,' Col said loudly, as he scratched his nose.

Lew passed Col, but he was looking back at his boat.

''Allo, Clown,' Col called to his back.

Lew walked away.

His Lordship Lewis Thomas. How could you forget that one? Always there like a heat rash just to remind you what he did. Because of him Mum's done a flit, you had to put up with lovely Aunt Emma—the Spider Woman—and now you've got Fat Theo. But Lew's as dumb as a lizard, so dumb his minders give him Christmas every day because he can't get anything for himself. So dumb he probably doesn't know what he's done to you. Oh he's far worse than Fat Theo.

Col stood up and the gas cylinder rolled forward a little. He looked at the cylinder and frowned.

11

Then he placed his foot on the cylinder and nudged it. It moved, but he stopped it and waited.

Five minutes later Lew tottered unsteadily back into the car park, making odd clicking sounds with his mouth. He was carrying the boom of the catamaran, a sail, a coil of rope, a billy, a frypan, a large box of tins and groceries topped by a small tent. He looked like a walking landslide.

'Aren't you speaking today, Clown?' Col said.

Lew stopped, wriggled, caught the billy before it toppled and shuffled on. He wasn't trying to dance this time.

'Know where you can go, kid?' Col leant back and pushed the cylinder hard with his foot.

The cylinder crunched on the bitumen, picked up speed and rolled toward Lew.

Col heard two men strolling around the corner behind him. 'Watch out kid!' he yelled. 'You're going to get bowled!'

A tall yellow-haired man in uniform stepped past Col, turned from the fat, unshaven man beside him and shouted. Two seagulls squalled into the air from lazy perches on posts, and Lew stopped and watched them in curiosity.

The cylinder rumbled loudly across the bitumen and hit Lew. It swept his feet from beneath him, throwing the tent into his face, clipping his ear with the boom and exploding the tins and the groceries from the box in a wide arc. Lew fell hard to the concrete, winding himself and cracking his head as his load crashed, bounced and tinkled about him.

Col threw his head back and roared with laughter.

The fat man's face twitched around a smile but the

yellow-haired man glared at him and Col before striding toward Lew.

'Bloody idiot,' Fat Theo muttered. 'You get into the boat, Starkey. And stay there.'

Col saw the man in the police uniform and stopped laughing immediately. He stepped over Lew's sprawling body and reached the steps before he was stopped.

'Starkey!' the yellow-haired man shouted. 'I want you!'

'Didn't do anything, Sarge, really,' said Col, quickly.

'Come on, Sergeant, give the lad a go.' Fat Theo sounded bored as he pulled Col behind him. 'I saw the whole thing. That cylinder just started rolling by itself. You want to check how they stow things on the wharf.'

'I even shouted to warn him, didn't I?' said Col.

'A real couple of beauties, aren't you?' said Sergeant Austin, but he didn't stop Col hurrying down the steps to the speedboat.

'It was an accident, Sergeant,' said Fat Theo. 'You the kid's fairy godmother or something?'

'Just take care, Theo. I'm watching you.'

The fine network of red lines on Theo's cheeks flared. He half closed his small eyes as he followed Col ponderously to the boat and he whipped the bow line from a post as if he was about to hit someone with it.

'You handled him real great,' said Col, a little nervously.

Theo reduced the stern mooring line to a hand-held loop with a jerk that rocked the boat. He sat on the edge of the cockpit and swung himself behind the wheel.

'You are a pain,' he said.

'Ah, that kid gets me.'

Theo pressed a button to kick the big motor alive. 'Why did you have to bring the cops down on us? And to do it today . . .'

The speedboat slid past the catamaran and down the rock channel to the sea.

'Austin couldn't catch a bank robber in a wheelchair.'

'Well you'd better hope he doesn't catch us out there, because now he's going to try.' Theo pushed the throttle forward.

The boat pushed from the Australian mainland and aimed for the scattered Whitsunday Islands and the Great Barrier Reef. The stern dropped slightly to sit on a long ridge of churned water, as the bow lifted to show a curve of painted teeth.

'What's that kid to you, anyway?' said Fat Theo.

Col looked back at the shrinking wharf and the sergeant squatting before the sitting boy. 'Nothing. But I got him, didn't I?'

2

Sunbird

Sergeant Austin reached out to steady the boy as he pushed himself up from the bitumen. 'How are you, Lew?'

Lew's mouth sagged open as he swayed his head away from the sergeant. He saw the speedboat creaming from the creek and blinked at it.

The sergeant clicked his teeth and squeezed Lew's shoulder until the boy turned to look at his face. 'You all right?' he said slowly and precisely.

Lew frowned and his lips groped across his teeth, as if searching for a sound. 'Ay im . . .' He stopped, frowned and tried again. 'I am fayne, think you Brian.' His voice was high and a little strange, like wind passing through wire rigging, and he gestured as he spoke, to make sure the sergeant understood.

'Okay.' Brian nodded. 'Stand up?'

Lew rocked himself to his feet and surveyed his scattered gear. 'Col?' he said.

'Think so. But I didn't see it. Don't you be starting trouble, now.'

'Me?' Lew pointed at himself and his eyes widened.

Brian grunted. 'Let's see what you lost.' He began placing tins in Lew's battered box.

Lew collected the sailing equipment and humped it on his shoulder. 'Nat so bid,' he said.

'Not so bad?' Brian held up a dripping carton of eggs.

'Scrumbled iggs,' Lew said with a shrug. 'I wall eat thum tonight.'

'You off to the island?' Brian placed the carton carefully in the box and passed it to Lew.

'Yus. I hive some frens to see.'

'How long?'

'Maybe two wiks. Ay don't know.' Lew moved toward the steps.

'Well you just be careful, okay?'

Lew stopped on the first step and smiled back at Brian. 'You visit mi, kay? We hev speshul reef trout, maybe.'

'We'll see. Take it easy.'

Lew nodded and almost jogged down the steps to the landing and his small yellow catamaran. He placed all his supplies, equipment and the paddle on the trampoline deck close behind the mast, and stretched fine black netting over the lot. He tied the netting tightly to form a large sausage across the deck. Everything would get wet but the sun would fix that within an hour of landing.

He made several odd whistling sounds as he locked the boom to the mast and to the mainsheet, the soft orange rope that controlled it. He connected the mainsail to the wire halyard, but then left it alone, a collapsed tent on the taut trampoline deck.

The sergeant leant on a post and watched the boy push the catamaran easily from the sand and bounce aboard. Lew waggled the twin rudders to move the cat slowly down the creek, tightened the jib, lowered the rudder blades in the deeper water and glided into the still bay.

He looked back, saw the sergeant standing in the car park and waved.

'Swap you,' Sergeant Austin muttered as he walked away to type out a report or three.

★ ★ ★

''Kay?' Lew said as he patiently threaded the leading edge of the mainsail into the groove of the aluminium mast. 'No. Ikay. No, oekay, okay, okay. Yas. Okay.'

He shrugged and let it be. To Lew speaking was as tricky as shooting at a target blindfolded, and it annoyed him. He knew when he was close to the target only when people's eyes stopped wandering, stopped looking for somewhere else to be. Of course with friends he didn't have to try so hard. Brian, kids at school, Mum and Dad, whatever, they had got themselves tuned to his words. Mum and Dad were nearly as good as the Flying Finger Mob.

That was what he had needed before. The Flying Finger Mob would take care of Col all right, drive him out of town. Little Leon would jump on his foot, Cindy would probably elbow him in the ear, Mick would throw him into Airlie Creek, and Max . . . well, Max could've shown them the star to aim him at. Once.

Lew corrected his steering to point the cat at a black-hulled schooner anchored in the centre of the bay.

He supposed he had made a lifetime enemy in Col, or his nose had made an enemy. But Col had started picking on him the moment he'd heard his funny words at Proserpine School, so it didn't really matter. When

17

you smell smoke you have to do something about it. So Col can go and chase frogs.

Lew prepared to pull on the rope end of the main halyard and felt a sudden touch of excitement.

He stopped and frowned.

He was excited because there was no hassle for the next two weeks? No more Col, no maths, no awful English, no more mowing the lawn?

No.

Because he was getting back to the island? Again? After all these times?

No. Because of the sail.

Lew hauled on the halyard and a large white dacron sail with a bright emblem swept up the mast, caught a faint breeze and jerked the boom up and away from the deck. He made fast the halyard on the mast, tugged the orange sheet, and the main stiffened. The emblem became the black silhouette of a lonely gull against a deep red sun, almost covering the width of the sail.

Oh, it's good. It's very good.

And it was very good not only because it hinted at mysterious voyages, but because Mum had painted it. Now, at last, Mum was declaring that the catamaran might not be that bad after all.

Mum had fought Dad constantly over the cat ever since they had first seen it in a neighbour's yard. 'How can he sail something like that?' she said, or he thought she said. 'He'll drown.'

'How can he *not* sail it?' he said. 'Here's something he can do as well as the other kids.'

That was when Lew slid behind the other kids for another year, and Dad didn't really believe that as he said it and Lew didn't believe it either. But they tried. It was tough then, with Dad sitting beside him and

18

shouting, trying to tell him what everything was called and what to do ten seconds after it should have been done. He'd capsized the cat so many times Dad had gone sailing wearing only his swimming togs. But then he was allowed to sail by himself, and it worked. He could see the sails working, the wind on the water and he began to understand.

Dad said the worst part was when he stood on the beach and watched Lew sail further and further away and he could not call him back. But now he had no capsizes at all, even in a squall.

Then the longer voyages, Daydream Island, South Molle. 'This is madness!' Mum said, and he was getting nervous. He wouldn't have minded being given a limit, but Dad said: 'Let him go. Makes up a little for things.' So, on a fine day Whitsunday Passage had to be crossed. To Whitsunday Island, Hook Island, Cid, Hayman, Dent, Hamilton, Haslewood, and finally *his* island.

That was years ago. Through storms, blinding rain, calms, he had never been in trouble. Not seriously. So when Mum asked for the cat's mainsail and painted a setting sun and a wandering gull on it she might have been saying that she had stopped worrying. Much. Sail on, sailor.

Lew caught the name Night Hawk on a schooner as he scooted past her and decided that now his cat deserved a name. Roadrunner, Islander, Sunbird. Sunbird.

The cat caught a fresh breeze past the last of the anchored yachts, tilting a fraction and swirling a longer wake. Lew shifted and watched the sails straining together. Twin glassy waves gleamed at the bows and slid past the deck.

Okay. Sunbird.

Lew sat back, rested his hand on the aluminium bar of the tiller and aimed the cat between the tourist outpost of the Mandalay Coral Gardens, his last contact with the mainland of Australia, and distant Hayman Island, almost the northern edge of the Whitsundays.

His eye caught a large blob rising above Mandalay and he realized he was watching a light plane flying in from Whitsunday Island. The air was that clear. No, nobody flies from Whitsunday. The plane was flying from the blue and brown patterns of the Barrier Reef, a very early flight, but what a day . . .

He began to feel the discomfort of the gravel-rash from the fall onto his palms, and washed his hands in Sunbird's wake.

He was going to forget about Col for two weeks. For two weeks he and all the others who thought he was about as bright as a spangled drongo and shouldn't be trusted in a bath, let alone on a cat at sea, just didn't exist.

For two weeks he could almost forget about being deaf.

3

Red Shark

Col gripped the wheel as Red Shark hurtled from a low swell to crash on the back of the next, bouncing his air tank solidly in the bottom of the boat. He heard Theo grunt behind him, but concentrated on steering as the boat slid sideways and leapt forward again.

'Right?' he yelled.

Theo reeled forward from the motor he had been adjusting and fell into the passenger seat. 'Yeah,' he said.

Too bad, thought Col.

'How's it feel now?' Theo watched the tumbling forests of Whitsunday and Hook Islands separate and slip past, but he was listening to the beat of his motor. He had thought the tone of the 275hp motor had dropped a little as he passed the off-shore islands, Daydream and North Molle, and had been adjusting things since then.

'Good.' Col did not notice anything different about the motor, now or before, but he felt it was a good thing that Theo was looking for trouble now, before they reached the Reef. He did not like Theo's boat and at times he was convinced it would drown him.

A stupid boat, he thought. Only good for speeding

about on a river or a lake, so Theo uses it in the open waters of the Whitsunday Islands and the Great Barrier Reef. And it can be rough out here, man, real rough. So he comes out with only one motor. Ask him what happens if the engine breaks down and he says: 'Won't break down if you look after it right.' So what was wrong with it just then? Ask him what happens if a squall flips the boat and he'll say: 'Won't flip if you drive it right.' Big man, knows everything there is to know, but he'll sink us, or get us caught.

'That's better now,' said Theo. 'Listen to her. Lovely.'

'Yeah,' said Col, and shrugged. What can you say to a man who puts rags in the bottom of a boat to protect the floorboards, who polishes the motor every fortnight, who paints teeth on the bow and calls the boat Red Shark? He wanted to forget about the boat and think about that gun-metal blue Chrysler he was going to get with the money from this job.

'Ah, you wouldn't know. Keep it in the middle.'

Hook Island's underwater observatory, looking like a lift well without the building, slid behind.

'I know enough.'

'You know nothing. Nothing at all. Give me the wheel.'

'Now?' The boat was bouncing wildly towards a space of little more than a hundred metres between Hook and Whitsunday Islands.

'Now.' Theo clamped a hand on the wheel and jerked his free thumb over his shoulder.

Col shook his head and slid out of the seat, kneeing the wheel as he went. The boat yawed, roared toward a cluster of rocks on the Hook shore and he began to yell. Theo whirled the wheel as he moved sideways

22

and the boat broadsided past the rocks into the open sea.

'Bloody hell,' Col said.

'I just should've left you with Aunt Emma. It would have been easier.'

'I was going to leave her anyway. Mean witch. I don't need anybody.'

'That's fine. Nobody needs you.'

'You want to do yer own swimming at the reef? I don't mind.'

'Just shut up, all right?'

Theo pointed the bow of the boat a little north of a mountainous little island, almost the last of the Whitsunday Islands, and let Red Shark settle in gentler swells.

Col fiddled with a long black box he had hauled from the shelf above his knee, and suddenly realized Theo was the last relative he had. Not the last living relative, but the last relative he could talk to. Show his face at Emma's place and she'd call the cops. Pops? Can't remember him at all now. Mum?

Col's face darkened.

When did you last call Laura Mum? When did she behave like one? No matter, she was around until that clown Lew fouled everything up. Why did he have to do that? Now all he had was Theo, not Fat Theo but Uncle Fat Theo. Now that was a bit of a laugh. Go on, laugh.

'You checked your tank?' Theo said, nodding at the scarred yellow cylinder under Col's feet.

'Don't worry.' Col pulled the rotational aerial from the top of the black box and flicked a switch.

'I'm not worrying. I'm not wearing it.'

'This direction finder is not finding anything.'

'It wouldn't. It's only good for about a kilometre and the reef is still 50 kilometres away. Put it away and don't wreck it.'

Col snorted, but put the black box away. He looked at the mountainous island and aimed a finger at the air above the granite peak that dominated the island. Then he smiled and reached for a long plastic-wrapped parcel stowed behind the black box.

'What d'you think you're doing with that?' said Theo in annoyance.

'See that black dot above Border Island?'

'Yes.'

'It's an eagle.' Flapping about like the Clown, thought Col.

'So?'

'Bang,' said Col.

Theo was silent for a moment then jabbed his finger at the shelf Col had taken the parcel from. 'I wonder. Do you *ever* think?'

Col reluctantly put the parcel back. 'What's wrong?'

'Oh, you'll only have Austin waiting for us when we get back, or maybe chasing after us. Can you just go to sleep or something until I have to use you?'

'Yes, uncle.'

'You call me that again and you'll be looking around for your head!'

Col sprawled in his seat, closed his eyes and smiled.

4

Sea Eagle

Bullet!

Lew caught the gust in the corner of his eye, a shivering of the water that swept toward Sunbird very fast, an invisible sea devil caught at full pounce. He quickly loosened the main and tried to guess the angle of the wind before it hit the cat.

Ah, go on, he thought, give us a hint. Pretty please.

The gust had been bottled up, heated high in a gorge on Mount Merkera and fired straight at Lew as he turned toward the sun and his nearest island. Gusts like this are called 'bullets' by yachtsmen, for their speed, their sudden attack and for the damage they can do. A bullet has been known to catch the bare mast of an anchored yacht and heave it down to the water, making the deck a wall, the cabin wall a ceiling, with bedding, plates, books and cutlery tumbling. Lew had seen this one more than a hundred metres away, but he could only guess what it would do.

The bullet swept across the last few metres from Sunbird's stern and slammed the sails almost broadside, heaving the mast violently sideways. The main ballooned, the boom jerked on the end of its sheet, the sheet stretched and trembled in a halo of flung spray, the jib flogged the tilted mast and one hull reared from the water.

Lew threw himself across the deck and lay along the side of the flying hull. He pushed on the tillers with his left foot and for a few seconds he was looking at the underside of the deck. The lower hull disappeared in a welter of surf, he felt the wind heaving beneath the deck and he prepared to jump clear of the capsize.

But Sunbird began to turn into the wind, the deck eased down and the mast swayed back into the sky. Lew sat up as he corrected his steering. He hauled in both sails and felt the hull rise beneath him again, but this time everything was under control. With one hull scarring the surface of the sea, Lew sat high above the water, leaned far back and shouted. He turned an ear to the wind and caught the rhythm of the wind and the rumble of the shout in his head.

For all of three minutes Lew felt he was flying, chasing eagles across the sky.

When the cat finally put both its hulls on the water Lew stopped grinning and forced himself to make a decision. Straight ahead, no more than a couple of kilometres away, was the northern tip of North Molle Island. Behind North Molle there was the broad Whitsunday Passage and the distant islands he was sailing for. The fastest trip to his island was round the northern tip of North Molle and straight across. But that would be just open water, nothing to see and possibly a trace of danger.

Lew sucked a tooth and watched his yellow bows slide across the calm green sea. All the time in the world, he thought, and turned toward the southern tip of North Molle, Daydream Island and Unsafe Passage.

He watched the big diesel cats surging out from

26

Shute Harbour, heavy with tourists and bound for their home islands and possibly the Great Barrier Reef. A little later the tall-masted Gretel, once a challenger for the America's Cup, heeled under a cloud of white sail and fled north; the blue two-masted yacht Nari slid toward Whitsunday Island and Cid Harbour. At this time in the morning there was a lot to watch, but nothing close enough to worry about.

Lew swept closer to Daydream Island, close enough to see freshly brown people nervously nudge the resort's bright cats from the beach and a family explore among the rocks.

Any closer and they are going to want to talk to you. No thanks.

Lew aimed for the Unsafe Passage.

He liked the names of the Whitsundays. Cid Harbour was like the Spanish warrior who fought the Moors, way, way back, and it had held a fleet of damaged warships after the Battle of the Coral Sea in World War Two; Whitehaven Beach was a beach of white sand so fine it squeaked; Mosstrooper Peak, *his* peak, was a slab of granite that looked like an angry soldier. Some islands seemed more like a party of mineral experts than tropical hideaways: Goldsmith, Blacksmith, Hammer, Locksmith, Tinsmith, Bellows, Ingot and Bullion and Forge Rocks. The reefs smelled of fish: Hook, Line, Sinker and Net, for instance. And the Unsafe Passage was unsafe only if you tried to get the QE2 through it.

He passed the bushy tip of North Molle Island and entered the Whitsunday Passage with scarcely a ripple. Before him now were the jungled mass of Hook and Whitsunday Islands and a broad reach of deep water. The wind was dropping as the sun warmed the sky, the cat was slowing in the longest, most tedious part of the cruise, and there was nothing he could do about it.

Well, Dad would like it, Lew thought.

Dad and Mum had pinched the cat a while back, before Mum had painted the main. There was hardly any wind so Dad had sprawled on the deck and sun-baked. But Mum kept on fiddling with the tiller and sails and saying: 'Is this all the thing ever does?' Dad gave up and went for a swim, but a wind sprang up and swept Mum across Airlie Bay before she learned to control the cat. She wouldn't come in for half an hour, but after that she started painting the sail.

Lew adjusted his sails, extracted some sandwiches from the deck-net and relaxed. He hoped he had enough wind to reach his island before sunset.

Now the Flying Finger Mob ought to come to the island. Get them there by water taxi and leave them for a week. Why not?

Dad had given the Flying Finger Mob that name after trying to keep up with their conversation for half an hour, and it had stuck. Lew, Mick, Cindy, Leon and Max were all deaf, although Leon could hear pretty well with his hearing aid on. They had met at a signing class, learning to talk with their hands, and got together often after school. Oh, they had their own friends—or all of them, except sad Max—but it was something special when they met. Suddenly they could speak with their mouths and their hands as fast as they could think, all speaking at the same time and still understanding each other perfectly.

A plump seagull landed on the tip of Sunbird's mast and Lew threw a crust at it. The bird watched the looping crust in boredom then toppled from the mast, plucked the crust from the air and flew off.

But hang on. Mick, now a fisherman as well as a football star, would want to fish in the bay and race around the beach as if it was the footy oval. Cindy, she was far gone in computer programming. She'd tramp over the island with her nose wrinkled saying, 'What's *this* for?' Leon, he'd bring his earphones, never goes anywhere without them. He'd bring his tranny and jazz about all over the place. And Max? In the old days he would have brought his great telescope and somehow heaved it to the top of Mosstrooper and hunted for comets. But that was in the old days, before the twitchy kids had found him. He couldn't come now.

Lew peered bleakly into the glinting water for a moment.

No, that's silly. No misery today. Sorry fellas, forget it.

As the morning became afternoon the water darkened and moved with a slow rhythm. The Passage was deep and broad now as Sunbird moved toward the peaks of Whitsunday Island. Lew had seen the landward side in morning shadow, black valleys and heavy jungles of misty mystery, but now the island shimmered drowsily in the long afternoon sun. The tiny bays held a few bright anchored yachts like pearls, the sea flashed at its feet and the mystery had gone to sleep.

To Lew, Whitsunday was a lot like the Tahiti he had seen in pictures, especially after he had explored some of it, seen the deep jungle, flaming orchids and cascading waterfalls. He had often wondered if Lieutenant James Cook had felt the same way when he'd sailed past the islands a few months after visiting Tahiti.

Oh, Whitsunday was a great island all right, but he had his own.

The tiny gap between the long arm of Whitsunday and the ranges of Hook Island steadily widened as the sun slid down to the blue haze of the mainland. Lew smiled. He was going to reach the island while there was still some light in the sky. Just.

But the water between the dark green islands was churning angrily, throwing up a seething barrier against him.

Tidal race, he thought and eased off his main.

The water in the Passage was now being pulled toward the narrow cleft by the moon, glancing from rocks and cliffs in a swirling rush. Sunbird slid into the troubled water and was hit by short high waves at the bows, the port hull and the starboard rudder at the same time. The sails flapped in confusion as the mast drew wild circles in the sky and the deck bucketed.

Perhaps it would be smarter to get out until this settles, Lew thought.

But he saw a group of people watching him from the pier next to the underwater observatory and kept going. He reared, plunged and sailed sideways, but the narrow pass edged closer until the black rocks were finally behind Lew. The sea stopped pounding Sunbird. The waves spread wide and flung her forward like a dart.

What were you worrying about?

Lew shrugged and tightened his sails again. Clear of the long shadows of Whitsunday and Hook the water turned smooth and silver, rolling quietly from the horizon and the Barrier Reef. Ahead of Sunbird a dark island with a granite peak sat in the sea like a great slumbering lizard.

Border Island. Lew's island.

Lew loosened the main and watched the approaching

island warmly. He could recognise the familiar parts of the island long before he actually saw them. There were the caves of Mosstrooper Peak, the coral reefs of Cataran Bay, the fine sandy beach, the look-out rock on the saddle, the rock arrow, the islet. The places he would dream about all the time he was at school.

And there was Joe.

Lew searched the sky over the island for a minute and then smiled. He cut off all the fat and some meat from one of the steaks he was carrying and stood in the stern of the boat. He steered Sunbird with his knees and held out his piece of meat.

'Joe!' he shouted, and waited.

The black spot kept circling far above the island for a long while, then it began to drop until Lew could see the red mark on its chest. Lew relaxed his arm until the big sea eagle had cruised to sea level, until it was close enough for him to see the hook of its beak. Then he held his arm out straight over the sea.

The eagle swept toward the boat, a great brown kite clipping the wavetops, and tilted. For half a second it was drawing a line in the water with one wing, tumbling Lew's hair with the other. Then the meat was gone. The eagle climbed back into the sky.

Lew sniffed at the lingering smell of salty feathers in the air and waved.

You're glad to see me back? I'm glad, too.

5

The Reef

'Got him!' Col stood in the back of Red Shark and pointed the radio direction finder as if it had a fish on the end. He actually smiled.

'You're going to pitch it in the sea any sec. Watch it.' Theo had been nudging Red Shark over the swirled pattern of the Reef for most of the afternoon now, and his temper was tossed and fried.

'See?' Col pushed the detector over his shoulder.

Theo nodded at the slowly blinking red light and relaxed a little. 'Okay, it's here. Want a medal?'

The smile disappeared as Col pulled the detector away.

'We've still got to find out where that half-wit of a pilot dropped it. Which way?'

Col jerked his thumb angrily behind Theo's head but he pointed the indicator to his right until the light stopped blinking. He moved it slowly back to his left and stopped where the blinking was strongest. 'That way.'

Theo nudged the throttle and Red Shark slid over a curling reef. Castles of vivid coral and delicate fingers of green weed reached for the hull.

'It's getting stronger. We'll have it in our hands any minute.' Col said.

'Don't spend it before you see it.'

'It's here. It's here. What can go wrong now?'

'Just about everything. Why don't you shut up and get on with your job.'

A finger of coral poked at the outboard motor, but the reef receded into the royal blue of deep water.

'It's here,' Col said doubtfully.

'You mean here? Straight down in the deep?' Theo threw the motor out of gear.

'A little bit back. But it's on this side of the reef.'

'I'll kick his head in.' Theo pounded his wheel. 'You can't work with the clowns they give you. You really can't.'

Col looked smug. At least Theo was attacking somebody else.

Theo turned Red Shark slowly and eased it back toward the reef. 'I told him, "Come in low, like you are sightseeing for the tourists,"' Theo muttered.

'I'll get the anchor,' said Col and moved toward the bow.

Theo ignored him. '"Just drop the bundle inside Net Reef because it is nice and shallow there." But can he do that, eh? Oh no, he can't get Net Reef. He can't get any reef at all.'

Col watched the red light until it was flashing frantically, then dropped the anchor. 'Got it.'

'He's so stupid he ought to stay honest.'

'We've got it,' Col repeated.

Theo snorted. 'Can you see anything?' He put the motor in neutral again and waited to see what the currents would do with the anchor and the boat.

Col peered into the clear water for a while, then shook his head. 'Better get down there, I suppose.'

'So get on with it. There's not much sun left.'

Theo satisfied himself that the anchor was holding and cut the motor while Col grunted into a rubber vest, huge yellow flippers, a lead belt, a face mask and a large metal bottle of compressed air. He sucked at the mouthpiece, screwed his nose and spat into the water.

'Jeez, that's crook,' Col said, but Theo was scanning the horizon for other boats. 'Air tastes of oil. Really does.'

'You want to clean up sometimes,' Theo muttered.

Col shrugged, replaced his mouthpiece and toppled easily into the water.

He allowed himself to sink slowly, watching the boat recede from him, a black shoe-print in a blue mist threaded with gold. For a few seconds he listened to the calm thunder of his breathing, then he turned to the reef.

He liked diving. Turn your back on the push-push nigglers, Aunt Emma, Sergeant Austin, his worship the headmaster and Fat Theo, and they weren't there. Had never been there. No more: 'How dare you come into my house reeking like a brewery?' 'Starkey, I want you!' 'You're a vandal and a firebug, Starkey. You're out. Today.' 'You want a medal?' None of them could follow him now.

Col dipped toward the reef. He had been diving outside coral reefs for more than a year now, but he still felt that he was shrinking as he sank. A bright ribbon of small yellow fish swirled past his legs, but beyond them a giant's playroom shimmered in shadow. A crowd of heavy brain corals were stacked like huge basketballs, their maze of winding ridges attracting some lazy parrot fish. Great plates of staghorn coral stretched out into the dark water for up to two metres and a red-veined coral looked like a metre-high butterfly

34

with folded wings. A giant clam seemed to ripple its thick blue lips as Col passed and two red, blue-spotted coral cod dwarfed Col's flippers.

They had always been on his back, the nigglers. They never left him alone. Jackson, the headmaster, had been the worst, worse even than Aunt Emma. Always the little digs: 'Pity your father didn't stay, Starkey, to straighten you out.' 'I feel sorry for Mrs Starkey, having to hold that house together alone.' 'She must be proud of you, the greatest lout in the town.' Jackson was very lucky that he didn't get his house burnt instead of the school.

Col remembered the afternoon in the store room. Spilled paint and turps, rags and a flung match. He had watched the flames climb a wall and turned to run— into Jackson and half the school led by the Clown doing his hound-dog act.

Col shoved Jackson out of his head as he hovered over a deep chasm. He could not see anything beyond swaying weed tendrils, coral horns and scurrying fish, but there were clues if you looked long enough. To his left something had crashed through the delicate grey twigs of a clump of staghorn coral and below it a rock showed a fresh scar of flaring pink.

Col aimed himself like a torpedo and thrust his body between the brittle growths of horn that guarded the chasm. Dark green pennants of weed swept across his face as the chasm twisted and darkened.

He was constantly looking for more signs of a plummeting object, but he almost swam past the box. It was the same colour as the surrounding grey coral and partly covered by black weed, but Col glimpsed a corner of straight edges. A corner just doesn't exist on a reef. He drifted back to the box and nodded at it in triumph.

He felt ten thousand dollars richer.

It was the shape of a small suitcase, but deeply plunged into coral. It was battered, scarred and a little warped, but it was made of iron. It had been chosen to survive being dropped from a plane without a parachute over shallow water covering a coral reef, and it had survived. All Col had to do was to get the box to the boat so Theo could deliver it to the Big Man in Shute Harbour.

Col thought of the car he would buy, the gun-metal Chrysler, as he gripped one of the box's handles and pulled. The box did not move.

But maybe you're not thinking right. You could take all ten, and tell them all just where to go. You won't need Fat Theo any more, just try your luck on the Gold Coast. And if you take the box, the whole box, and run, you get the whole box of dice. You are rich, man, never have to think of working again for years and years.

Col placed his flippers on either side of the box and heaved, bubbles streaming past his jaw. Fragments of coral tore from under Col's flippers and cascaded lazily toward the sandy bottom.

Not moving at all. Maybe jiggle it a little. Anyway how're you going to get the whole box, eh? Theo's got the boat, the Big Man wants the box and he makes Jackson look like Santa Claus. Forget it.

A large piece of coral hit the sandy bottom and the sandy bottom moved.

Col jerked at the box in a swirl of small red fish, dislodging more coral but hardly lifting the box.

A large oval of mottled sand, beached weed and

shadow slid over a flat rock and flipped an angry tail in the dark.

Come on, come on! Why don't you just— Wobbegong!

Col swayed away from the box as he saw the shining brown eyes watching him, the mock seaweed sprouts framing the mouth and the flat head. The Tasselled Wobbegong looked like a throwaway rug, but it was at least two metres long. Col knew that Wobbegongs were only interested in small fish, but they have been known to bite at divers when angry. And they *were* sharks, weren't they?

Col left the box imbedded in coral and slowly pushed himself toward the surface, watching the Wobbegong until it was masked in shadow. He felt a strengthening current as he neared the boat and found himself swimming diagonally to reach it.

'Find it?' Theo was sprawled in the back of the boat, his hair glowing white in the setting sun.

Col nodded and pushed his mask to the top of his head.

'Well, where is it?'

Col unbuckled his lead belt, threw it into the boat and began to take off his air bottle.

'What are you doing kid? The job's gotta be done.'

'There's a shark down there.' The air bottle slid heavily over the side.

'What sort of shark?'

'Wobbegong,' Col muttered and kicked himself out of the water.

'Wob—?' Theo laughed for a long time. 'You mean that?'

'It's big and it's mean. *You* go down there.'

'What are you, a bloody sis?'

'The box is stuck in the coral. I'll go down with a rope later and you can pull it out. No worries.'

'Why later? Why not now? Frightened of a nibble from a wobble?'

'Can't you hear it?'

Theo frowned and listened. There was the sound of water rippling over pebbles in a shallow creek.

'We're in a channel and the tide's going out.'

'So?'

'So I don't know how long I gotta be down there, but it gets hairy down there with a lagoon emptying on to you. You can get cut up real bad.'

'You can get cut up real bad up here . . .'

'Look we wait a few hours, we know where it is and we pull it up like a dead fish. What are you worried about?'

'And maybe your terrible fearsome shark is gone then?' Theo shook his head, but he looked at the bare knuckles of coral breaking the still water on both sides of the boat. He could see a broad dent in the surface of the sea and hear the ripple increase to a rush.

'All right,' said Theo. 'We wait.'

6

Cataran Bay

The wind had died to a faint touch on the cheek by the time Lew glided into Cataran Bay. Sunbird was quiet now, the hulls sitting steady and the rudders tracing faint lines on the polished water. Lew rose awkwardly to his feet beside the motionless sail and stretched.

He looked about him and noted with deep satisfaction that he was alone in the bay. No tourist cruiser, schooner, ketch, family yacht, not even a dinghy. Border Island was his again.

It hadn't changed. It never did. To his left Moss-trooper Peak rose dark and almost sheer to 218 metres, home for eagles, topped with a king's throne. To his right a small cove hid between cliffs and under a patch of tropical forest, a refuge for herons, green ants and shallow water coral. Ahead was the saddle, running from Mosstrooper to the rest of the island, a sculpture garden for the wind. And below the saddle the straight stretch of sandy beach—his beach, his thinking spot, his stage.

The beach, the island, were still unmarked by people, apart from the wooden signs announcing that this was Border Island and don't leave a mess.

Lew steered to the right of the beach with his foot.

Here a tidal creek had pushed the sand aside, allowing the tide to flow past rain-carved rocks and small trees. The creek was now a shining finger of the bay.

All the way, Lew thought.

Sunbird slid past the main beach, scudded over a large flat stone and stopped on a sand-bar. Lew furled the jib, pulled down the main and stepped out on to the beach. He worked his toes into the coarse sand as he looked over the unmarked beach at the water. The bay was beginning to reflect the still fire of tropic dusk in the sky.

She'll do, he thought. But we only just made it in time.

He stripped and sprinted back into the bay, allowing the water to trip him. He turned his fall into a long dive and swam powerfully twenty metres from the shore. He stopped a moment, swept his hair back from his forehead, breathed deeply and dived.

Lew loved swimming underwater more than anything else in the world. Even more than sailing with one hull in the air, or having an eagle as a sort of mate. And swimming underwater off Border Island was the top of the world.

He stroked past the swaying purple fingers of a colony of anemones, bustling with the white-slashed dusky anemone fish, twisted and chased a school of the small blue pullers until they dodged between and under staghorn corals.

Maybe diving was great because while he was down here he was equal to anybody and better than most. Underwater nobody has ears, just eyes. Maybe, or maybe he just liked chasing fish among the coral.

He was eyed by a worried striped thicklip, so he eyed it back in polite conversation.

Maybe he wished he was a fish.

Oh, not the gleaming speed merchants like the white pointer shark, you understand, or the ones that spend all their time lying on the sand waiting for food to swim along, like the stone fish. And definitely not the delicious ones like the reef trout, always being hunted by other bigger fish and hungry fishermen. But perhaps an orange sea perch, small enough and quick enough to dive to coral for safety and smart enough to know when to dive.

But he wasn't a fish. Reluctantly Lew turned at the bottom of the bay and kicked for the surface. He breathed a little, looked at the darkening hoop pines marching up from the rocks on the side of the bay, and dived again.

The bay seemed all right this time. The last time Lew had come to his island he had had to spend a day cleaning cans and bottles from the bottom and he could see where coral outgrowths had been snapped off for souvenirs. There had seemed to be fewer fish, or more frightened fish that time, but there was no sign of visitors now. That was good. He could even stop wishing for an invisible fence around the island.

Lew surfaced and swam ashore. The beach was now a silver line in the darkening gloom of the island and he thought he had better prepare for the night. He looked at the yellow moon drifting above his head as he dried himself and decided against the tent. He half-buried his gas burner in the coral sand and scrambled the broken eggs he had brought from Airlie Beach.

Nice of Col to help with the meal, he thought with a half smile. But I would've gone for a steak instead.

As he fried two slices of bread in a little butter a small cloud of electric-blue butterflies hovered above the flame, the fire glowing through their wings as if they were gauze.

A midnight black crow pranced up before Lew, tilted its head and fixed him with a single eye.

Oh, it's you, Crusoe.

Crusoe because the bird had seemed to be an unhappy castaway crow every time Lew had seen it.

Crusoe took a bold step forward.

Bet you've been screaming for food for ten minutes, eh? Forgot it was me, and you had to play by my rules.

Crusoe bounced to within a metre of Lew's feet.

Lew said, 'G'day,' and threw a crust to the crow. Crusoe caught the crust and examined it.

Lew placed a billy of water on the burner for a cup of tea and for washup water.

Crusoe was like Max.

Lew stopped with his hand on the billy.

What? Like Max, always hanging about for a crust.

Lew fanned his fingers at the crow raised an eyebrow and cocked his head like a cartoon plotter.

'What you doing, Lew? Where you going, Lew? What're you thinking, Lew?' No, really. Max hung about anyone, anyhow, just because you let him hang around.

Crusoe stared at Lew for a second then pecked at the crust.

All right, all right, he wasn't that bad. Just seemed that way sometimes. Maybe because of his folks. Lovely pair they are, him with his itty-bitty moustache (Lew walked pompously away on his knees with a finger hooked below his nose) and her wearing all the badges and always carrying the Terribly Important briefcase (he waddled back to Crusoe).

42

Crusoe thrust his head forward and clicked his beak.

The telescope? Oh, yeah, it was great. He could get all the rest of the Flying Finger Mob hunting for stars on Scrubby Hill. For a while he was the Big Cheese. 'There's Betelgeuse, the red star, and Saturn and—I've got Jupiter, Lew, I've found Jupiter!'

Lew clapped his fists together over his left eye and writhed on his back in the sand as he hunted for stars in the deep blue sky.

Crusoe flew off.

All right, don't listen. His folks didn't. Just kept on pretending that he wasn't deaf. 'Oh, dear Max is perfectly all right, just dreamy. Aren't you Max?— kick, kick—Psst, let's give Max a super telescope and pretend he's not here at all.'

Lew shook his head and poured hot water into his mug.

I suppose Max just had to hang around us like a great damp blanket. There wasn't anyone else. Except his twitchy mates. Come on, leave him alone.

Lew finished his meal slowly and threw the remnants of a crust far out into the bay, watching as it was torn apart by fish.

Crusoe is not like Max and Max is not here. Go away Max. Sorry Crusoe. Crusoe is like the Swiss Family Robinson, or Ben Gunn of Treasure Island. All castaways with an island to rule. If Joe the eagle doesn't mind. But now the island was his. For a couple of weeks he was going to do exactly what he wanted, when he wanted to do it. Like Crusoe.

Lew scrubbed the plate with coral sand then washed it and the frypan with hot water and soap. He set the tea aside, poured hot and cold water into a basin and washed the salt from his body.

He wondered about why there seemed to be more dusky anemone fish near Mosstrooper and fewer blue puller in the centre of the bay as he unrolled his groundsheet on the sand. Did they affect each other? Why? Why is the hoop pine on the south slope drooping? Are termites getting at it from inside? That's the trouble with having an island to yourself. You have to worry about it.

Lew smiled and set his sleeping bag on the groundsheet. No need for a tent tonight. He lay back, sipped his tea and stared up at the barely moving black silhouettes of the hoop pines and the cold blaze of the galaxy sweeping across the sky. A great night for Max and his telescope.

Lew frowned and shook his head. Not Max again.

Suddenly a bright green pinpoint of light flashed before his nose, flashed again and glowed for several seconds. It dimmed as it moved along a thin twig into the starlight. Firefly.

That's the thing about the island. It's got Crusoe the Crow, the eagles Joe and Josie, a bay full of fish and coral, green ants and fireflies glowing in the night. Everything on the island is moving, growing, alive.

There's no room for Max on the island. Because Max is dead.

7

The Box

It sounded like a waterfall now. A waterfall so big, so near that Col could not hear Theo's motor throbbing, and it made him nervous.

If he closed his eyes he felt as if he was lying on a rock with a river thundering past his head, rattling boulders in its bed, cascading down a misty slope and leaping into space. And his rock was moving, sliding toward the boiling water . . .

It wasn't much better if he kept his eyes open. The reef by his side had become a ragged black wall, the anchor rope was stretched taut into the swiftly running current, and Theo was running his motor against the current in case the anchor pulled loose. He could see the break in the reef only fifteen metres away, flashing white as the lagoon on the other side of the reef poured out its water in a desperate attempt to catch up with the receding tide.

This tidal race had gone on twice a day for thousands of years. Col knew that. It was as monotonous as sinking a jug in the sea and then emptying it, sinking, emptying, sinking . . . but the rush of the water would not let him relax.

Col lay in the back of the boat, stared at the rocking, lurching stars and waited.

★ ★ ★

'Time's up.'

Col was shouting at Aunt Emma, a blotched scarecrow of a woman with a righteous tongue, when the image quivered. He had started to call her Spider Woman because she looked, moved and sounded like one. Maybe she had heard him, and she went on whining away about how useless he was. That was all right, she always went on like that, but she had started to tell him how useless his mother was. Who did this dried-out old witch think she was? She lived in this stinking shack in a winos' lane and she tried to set herself up as some sort of a judge . . .

'Come on, Starkey.'

Col felt a nudge on his leg. He shook the Spider Woman out of his head and reluctantly sat up. Everything was still now; the motor was quiet, the boat drifted near the black shadow of the reef and the waterfall was now a slow eddy in the moonlight.

'Even you can't complain about this. Can you?'

'Be better in the morning . . .'

'Look boy, I've been fiddling with the boat half the night just keeping us where we ought to be. I'm not going to waste any more time talking. Just get over the side and work.'

Col slid into the water ten minutes later without a word to Theo.

Theo passed him the torch and a rusty hatchet with a warning: 'Keep the light pointed down, right? All the time. I don't know what they've got up there,'— thumbing at the sky—'but we don't want them to

46

know what we've got down here.' He began to feed out the line attached to Col's belt.

Col pressed his mouthpiece and mask into place, pushed himself from the boat and sank.

The moon followed him down for less than an armstroke, then he was alone, drifting in the black. He could feel slight currents moving hair on his arms, but beyond that there was nothing.

What if he got under a coral ledge and lost the torch? He wouldn't be able to find his way out. He would be trapped down there, him and the shark . . .

Don't be stupid!

The torch flared in the dark, catching a school of white fish in the flick of a tail. Col squeezed the handle and checked the cord loop round his wrist. He blew a rush of bubbles past his mask and followed the beam down.

The reef itself was awake now. The polyps, the tiny animals that built the reef with billions of their shells, had stretched their tiny tentacles to catch organisms in the water. What had been pink coral balls during the day was now a mass of yellow wildflowers in the misty light. Fish darted across Col's mask as if in a hurry to catch a meal or to avoid becoming one.

But the box had not moved. Col slowed his descent and probed the depths beyond the box for any sign of the Wobbegong but the shark, grazing as patiently as a cow in a large paddock, had moved on. It might be back in a month, depending on currents and the drift of the fish, but it would not trouble Col tonight.

Col untied the cord from his belt and looped it through one of the handles on the box. He struck at the corals around the box with the hatchet a few times but he could not get enough force through the water.

He braced himself and jerked the cord very hard twice, then swam away. He saw the cord tighten as Theo hauled on it, then heard the buzz of the motor. The cord quivered, coral shifted and tumbled from under the box, but the box did not move.

Weak boat, thought Col. Red Shark? Pink Parrot Fish.

The buzz in the water stopped and the cord sagged. Col watched the box, the line, his watch and a Red Emperor catch and swallow a small regal angel fish.

He shrugged and tried to lever the box from the coral with the hatchet, but he found himself swinging around the box and the box not moving at all. And he had to keep an eye on the drifting cord because he did not know what Theo would try now, or when.

What's he doing? Fat blob, doesn't he know I'm running out of air?

The cord began to lift again, slowly, as if the boat was drifting with the tide.

He's pulled the anchor up; that's what he's done.

The water buzzed again, louder, angrier this time. The cord leapt as if there was a great fish on the end, straightened and quivered.

The rope's going to break, Col thought. What are we going to do then?

The buzz suddenly changed and the cord lurched from the reef, coiling freely in the open water before it flowed after the buzz. It took Col a moment to realize that the box was out of the coral and climbing toward the surface.

He waved the hatchet triumphantly at the box as it passed him. Then he thrashed after it.

What if he keeps on going? He's got everything, just

pull up the box and take off for Shute Harbour. Leave you here. Nobody'd know and he'd do it too.

But the buzz quietened and Col was able to catch the box with ease, coming up with it as Theo dropped the anchor again.

'What do we do now?' Col said.

'Turn the light off,' Theo growled. 'You're a bloody lighthouse.'

Col fumbled at the torch, blazing at the sky, until it died.

'What we do now is nothing.' Theo pulled the heavy box over the side with a grunt. 'Until these stinking reefs get covered again, we wait.'

8

Trout

Lew rolled out of his sleeping bag before the sun touched the sky. He walked across the beach to the water's edge half asleep and fell in.

His first thought was: This is going to be a great day.

He surfaced and wondered why.

The last handful of stars over his head was being washed by a warm blue haze, a single strand of high cloud was touched by a dull fire, Joe was circling the sky and the air was as still as a glass table.

We may have something here, he thought.

He swam back to the beach, dried, pulled on his shorts, wriggled into his ragged sandshoes and stopped.

Nothing's moving but me.

Crusoe glided across the beach and settled a metre from Lew.

Nothing but me and him.

Lew grabbed a long stick and stood up. Crusoe stepped warily sideways, but Lew twirled the stick and walked past the bird on to the beach.

Crusoe and Thursday Afternoon surveying their island. No, the island has not sunk or been invaded by cannibals. All's well.

Crusoe walked unhappily after Lew for a few steps, then stopped.

No breakfast, big deal boss man. Get your own. No shout at me. I am not listening.

Lew picked up pieces of seaweed and placed them on his eyebrows and his lip. He twirled his stick and waddled away, Charlie Chaplin on a lonely beach. He climbed imaginary steps, fought an imaginary foe, danced with an imaginary girl. He bowed to Mosstrooper and then to Crusoe.

Crusoe cocked his head, ruffled his feathers and scudded to a distant rock.

Critics, always critics, thought Lew. All right, be serious. Breakfast.

Lew collected his fishing gear and pulled Sunbird against the ripple of an incoming tide to the bay. This time he completely ignored the folded sails and paddled smoothly out of the bay to the open sea. A long while ago Lew had decided to do all his fishing away from his island. Any fish that had found its way to Cataran Bay was in sanctuary. He would watch it, maybe even chase it, but he would not catch it. So he caught all his fish in open water.

Anyway, they were bigger.

Lew unwrapped the prawns he had brought from Airlie Beach, carefully threaded one of the biggest on to his hook and threw it over the side. He held the cork cylinder very loosely in his hand and allowed the weight of the lead ball and the hook to pull the line gently through his fingers.

He was fishing for breakfast, but lunch would be fine. He was in no hurry at all.

To his left the sky lightened as the northern edge of Mosstrooper flashed and glittered, greeting the sun on the horizon. Ahead the purple shadows of distant Hook Island faded into the rich greens of the forest, making the island seem so close he felt he could swim to it. The sea was so still his island—the peak, the bay and the lizard body—was beginning to look like a roast duck on a silver plate. Something he could pick up and slide about, and he was only half a kilometre from the bay. Joe drifted far above the peak, an eagle asleep on a column of rising air.

Lew didn't want to see any other boat, or plane, or anyone anywhere. His island? Just now he owned the planet.

The line twitched in Lew's fingers.

Already?

For an instant Lew thought of ignoring the line, but only for an instant. He moved his fingers to feel the weight of the line, and waited.

Something began to nibble at the line and Lew swept his hand up over his head. He allowed the fighting weight to pull his arm down again, smiled and hauled on the line, hand over hand until he was knee deep in a glistening web. He could see a dark shape deep in the clear blue water, a flash of red, then he held a thrashing blue-speckled flame-red fish almost as long as his arm.

Coral trout, he thought. Breakfast, lunch and dinner.

He planted his sandshoe on the fish, freed his hook and pushed the fish into the empty net behind the mast. The sun lifted from the sea to tint the water and redden his arms while he carefully rewound his line, but he paddled lazily back into the shadow of the peak before he felt the heat. There was just enough water in the creek to float Sunbird back to his private pool.

Lew wrapped the trout and a halved tomato in aluminium foil and grilled them in their own juice, while he prepared a simple salad. He found it very hard to stop himself from dribbling as the aroma of the cooking fish wafted across the warming beach from the gas stove.

Mum should be here.

He looked up in surprise.

Mum? Give it a go.

He pulled the aluminium from the flame on a spatula, but singed his fingers a little as he unwrapped the fish and was engulfed in a wave of rich steam. He sucked his fingers until they stopped throbbing, then plunged a fork into the fish.

Yes, Mum. Forget about the Flying Finger Mob, Mick, Cindy, Leon racing over the beach like cannibals looking for lunch, and Max looking for something to steal. Forget him anyway. If Mum comes you get Dad, of course. Dad's all right at home, great at home, but get him here and he'd just want to fish in the bay. Get Mum here on a day like this and she'd stop thinking her kid goes through hurricanes to get to a muddy rock full of snakes. She'd get her paints out and put Mosstrooper on canvas. And Cataran Bay, Joe, maybe even the view from the throne.

He peeled the spotted red skin from one side of the trout.

But get her here and it won't be like this. It'll change, it'll blow, it'll rain for days and days and she'll never let you get anywhere near here again. Scrap that idea. Sit here and eat and eat until you get fat.

Lew dipped the skin in the tomato juice and ate it with his eyes closed. Then he began to attack the fine white flesh, hot, juicy and with a delicate tang.

There might be a better tasting fish in the world, but

he couldn't think of it. Not this morning, not here on this beach, anyway.

Lew stopped eating with a guilty shock a little later as he realized he had eaten one side of that huge fish, from the eyeball to the tail, and was about to turn it over. He had ignored the salad.

He could imagine Mum standing on the sand, one hand on her hip and a mean look in her eye. 'Your greens, boy! Your greens!'

Another reason for keeping Mum off his island.

He nibbled at a lettuce leaf, then put the salad and the remains of the trout in a plastic box. He dug a hole in the wet sand and buried the box—almost like having a handy refrigerator—threw the fish skeleton to the nibblers in the bay, washed up and cleared his beach.

Except, let's face it, Mum would love this island and it deserved to be painted. Don't be an island miser. Dad would want you to sail him round the island, and why not? He'd probably capsize the cat again, but you have to put up with the old man sometimes, don't you? And the island would probably stand a raid from the fearsome Flying Finger Mob, even Max. No. Go away Max, beat it.

Lew packed his day pack, his old camera, a notebook, a biro, a battered pencil case, some biscuits and cheese.

Which Max?

Lew slung his bag on his back and hesitated.

Which Max? The one with the telescope and the star charts in his head, the Max that would climb Mosstrooper with the telescope on his back just for a clear night up there in the Milky Way? Or the Max who would come to the island to see what he could take home and sell? The Max with the new mates, strange mates, twitchy mates, huddle-in-the-corner mates? Which Max?

Lew settled his bag on his back and walked across the beach.

Doesn't matter. They're both gone.

Lew pushed Max off the island and refused to think of him again.

He took a last look at the sea and realized it was not moving at all. Oh, if you watched the tideline the water receded a few centimetres, rippled a little and crept back up the sand to leave a line of tiny bubbles. But the sea stretching from Lew's island to Hook Island might have been a sheet of polished metal, blue fading to white. He could see a single fish jumping five hundred metres away.

It's going to be a glasshouse, Lew thought. Wonder what it's like out there, on the reef . . .

Lew turned from the sea and began climbing toward the saddle.

9

Glasshouse

Col was burned awake by the sun sitting on his eyelids. He rolled and scraped his foot across Theo's jaw.

'Aw, get off!' Theo spat. Then. 'Oh, Gawd.'

Col sat up and the boat rocked in a sea of glass, sending slow ripples into the haze. The milky blue of the sea flowed into the milky blue of the sky so smoothly that there just was no horizon. The boat was the only solid thing in a great flawless crystal ball, with no up, no down, nothing at all.

'It's a glasshouse condition,' said Col, with a little awe.

'So we stick out like a sore thumb.' Theo wheezed into the front seat and started the motor. 'Get the anchor up!'

Col yawned, stepped over the seats and the windscreen and pulled on the rope. The boat moved sluggishly forward until the rope led straight down. Col grunted, braced himself and grunted again.

'Come on, come on!'

'It's stuck.'

'Stuck?'

'I can't get it up. It's caught on a hunk of coral or something.'

'Well, cut it off.'

'We could—'

'Cut the thing off!' Theo thrust a flashing fishing knife at Col.

Col shrugged and sawed quickly through the rope. Theo opened the throttle while Col was still on the bow, tumbling over the windscreen and into the back of the boat. The boat left an arc of hanging water and skidded toward distant Whitsunday Island.

'Fat fool,' muttered Col as he raised himself to a shaky knee.

'Eh?' shouted Theo. 'What you say?'

'Nothing. There's a plane.'

'Where?' Theo sounded alarmed.

'Oh.'

'What?'

Col had seen a small seaplane low in the sky far to his left. Then he saw a bigger black object with a mast, a boat, close to the plane. But this boat was drifting *above* the plane. Col rubbed his eyes and squinted.

'Hey, that's Hardy's Reef, the tourists,' said Theo. 'Where the hell are we?'

Col forced some understanding from what he was seeing. Okay, that's a seaplane, but it's not flying and that's not sky, it's sea. The plane is just delivering tourists to that boat there and the horizon is somewhere above all that. It was like getting kicked in the head.

Theo began to decelerate. 'I thought we were out of the reefs—'

Red Shark suddenly bucked, slewed and clattered. Col clutched for the rear of the seat, but the boat had shifted too far sideways for him to save himself. He hung spreadeagled in the air for a full second before he ploughed into the water.

He surfaced to see the boat wandering all over the water with Theo staring at his feet in horror and the motor coughing and shaking violently.

'Hey!' he shouted, a touch of panic in his throat.

Theo looked up in surprise and aimed the boat at him. 'I'm not stopping!' he shouted. 'You'd better grab hold when I go past.'

'The motor—' Col pointed wildly as he pictured the large propeller churning the water behind the boat. But it was too late. The boat was too close, too fast. He saw the severed anchor line flapping about the bow and reached for it as the boat nudged him aside.

He was swung hard alongside the boat, banged several times against the hull and felt the rope being pulled from his hands. He screamed into the foaming water, then he was being pulled into the boat by his belt.

'Okay, we got you. Why don't you stay in the damn boat? Now bail!'

Col raised himself groggily and realized that the bottom of the boat was awash. He picked up the bucket and started scooping water before he looked for the cause.

'What's happened?' He could see a deep gash in the hull directly beneath Theo, pouring bubbles into the green water in the cockpit.

'What d'you think happened, eh? We copped a bit of coral. We got a hole and we lost a blade—maybe more—from the prop.'

'Maybe we can plug it.' Col punctuated his words with buckets of water.

'What?'

'Plug it! Plug the hole!'

'Plug it with what?'

Col dropped the bucket and hurled a seat cushion at

58

the bubbling gash. He wrestled with the cushion, tore it apart on the jagged metal and thrust his arms into deepening water. Col stopped, knelt on the cushion and panted. 'Can't stop it. Just can't.'

'So get up and get on with the bailing.'

'Maybe we can make it to the tourist boat.'

'Oh you are a wonder. What're you going to do with the box?'

'All right!' Col's voice became shrill. 'What are *you* going to do? We're sinking! Can't you see?'

'See that little island just before Whitsunday Island?'

Col swallowed and stopped bailing for no more than a moment. The islands—all of the islands—seemed to be floating above the sea. The sea was a lake but the little island before Whitsunday was a very long way away. Maybe forty kilometres.

'We can't make it. No hope at all.'

'You want to tell that to the Big Man?'

Col heaved a bucket of water overboard and bent for another. He shook his head.

'We can make it. The water's not coming in so fast. You keep the water down. I'll keep the boat going. We get there, dump the box in the shallows, move on a bit and then we call up help. We come back for the box in a couple of days. Just bail.'

'Might as well jump now,' breathed Col as he tipped the bucket. 'We're going to be swimming before we reach Border Island anyway.'

10

Hideaway

Lew sat on a rock on the saddle and scratched his head. He knew all about freeze frames on TV. He had seen footballers caught in the air with two fingers on the ball, pole vaulters dangling upside down over the bar, the villain's car held the moment it leapt from a cliff, but he'd never been trapped in one before. It was weird.

He was stuck in the middle of a raging storm; his eyes told him that. A stunted palm before him was bent at right angles toward Cataran Bay. A bush had been clipped and formed behind the shelter of a clutter of boulders, looking as if it had been attacked by an enthusiastic gardener. Clumps of tenacious grass had been flattened and the single dark spears of the black-bows had been snapped below the seed pods. Above, caves and granite slabs gave Mosstrooper the deep lines of a man suffering in a hurricane.

Except there was no wind, no breeze, no wafting air at all.

On almost any other day the South East Tradewinds would be gathered in by the broad arms of the island and blasted across the saddle, hurling a flight of eagles into the sky. There were no trees, no free-standing bushes on the saddle because of the constant wind, and normally Lew would have to lean hard into that wind to walk here. The palm, the bush, the grass, would be much as they were now, but the blast from the sea would be making wild sense of it all.

But now Lew caught himself leaning from habit and he felt a funny little shiver when he stared at the deformed palm. He could look down into the bay and see the brown shadow of the coral beneath the water, even the dark mass of Mosstrooper reflected in the water. On the other side the sea was a glass table, stretching all the way to Haslewood Island near Whitsunday Island and out at sea he might even see the Barrier Reef.

He turned lazily and looked.

Not quite. Perhaps from the throne on Mosstrooper, but not from here.

Out at sea he could see deep, dark patches and the long line that marked a steady current flowing between the Whitsundays and the Reef area, but there was not a single ripple on the water. Not a cloud in the sky, not a tree, not a blade of grass lifting before a breath of air, nothing at all to make this morning feel *real* . . .

Wait, wait . . .

Just a small wake crawling across the sea like a limping water spider. A sick boat. A very sick boat.

Lew plucked a stem of grass and nibbled at it as he watched the boat stagger toward his island. He saw the shimmer of rising smoke well before he could pick out the crimson of the boat's hull.

It's going to die any moment now. Why don't they stop and fix it before it blows up?

Lew shielded his eyes.

It's Red Shark.

61

He allowed himself to smile. Disaster couldn't happen to better people. But the smile faded as the boat moved closer.

Someone's bailing. Are they sinking?

Lew threw his grass stem away and sat up. He felt guilty.

The motor seemed to be jerking about on its mountings and the boat slewed, as if it was trying to shake itself clear.

They aren't going to make it. Haven't they called for help on the radio?

Col—Lew recognized the humped, heavy figure now—stopped bailing and stared at the thickening smoke, swaying his body as if he was about to fall from the boat. Theo seemed to be shouting at him and he bailed again, slowly, and watching the motor all the time. Red Shark disappeared behind Mosstrooper and Lew waited for the boat to reappear near the bay.

When the boat rounded the rocks Lew stopped worrying and started feeling annoyed. From this moment his island was not his any more. Not only would he have to tolerate them, he would probably have to look after them, feed them until help came. Maybe even go and get help in Sunbird, even ferry them to the Hook Island underwater observatory, his nearest neighbour.

All this for the great nit that's been treating you like the village idiot. And don't forget that gas cylinder at Airlie Beach either. Why couldn't they they get into trouble somewhere else?

Theo took the boat into the bay, shattering the blue glass of the water and the dim images of the coral below. He jerked the motor's gear into neutral, stopping the crippled propeller. Col kept on bailing, spreading the rainbow stain of petrol and oil across the bay.

Lew jumped to his feet in anger. They can't do that!

He thought of shouting at them, but it would come out wrong, he was too far away and what good would it do anyway?

For sure he wasn't going to help them now. Not unless he really had to.

Col stopped bailing and leant against the back of a seat, his arms hanging limply by his side. Theo said something to him but he did not move. Theo then stepped over the seats and lifted a heavy box from between Col's feet, steadying it on the edge of the coaming as he looked very hard at the peak and sideways at Lew.

Lew took a step backwards and looked for a place to hide.

Theo pointed and shouted something to Col, who looked up.

This is stupid. They are just too far away to see anything up here.

But Lew half crouched, putting the right-angle palm between him and the boat. Over a frond he saw Theo sweep his hand away from him and back to Mosstrooper. Col sighted along Theo's arm as if it were a rifle and seemed to nod. Theo then tipped his dripping box into the bay.

Lew frowned and straightened again.

What *are* they doing?

Theo bailed furiously in the back of the boat for several minutes before he thrust the bucket in Col's hands and stepped back to the wheel. The engine coughed, roared and pushed Red Shark out of the bay, leaving a pall of smoke hanging over the water.

Oh, I just don't get it. They're still sinking. Why didn't they hit the beach? Doesn't make sense at all.

Red Shark turned right and shuddered behind Moss-trooper again. Ten minutes later it cleared the peak and crept very slowly toward distant Haslewood Island.

They won't make it. They're going to sink for sure this time.

Half an hour later the boat stopped, a tiny black speck half-way between Border Island and Haslewood. Lew imagined Theo and Col taking frantic turns in bailing, with Red Shark slowly going under. He wondered how long it would take him to reach Sunbird and paddle after them.

He relaxed when a bigger speck slid to Red Shark from the south—probably Sergeant Austin's boat—merged with it and stopped. After ten minutes the police boat moved off, leaving no trace of Red Shark.

Lew shook his head and walked down the rough-studded path to the bay. He couldn't work out what Theo and Col had been trying to do, but by the time he swung down to the flat on one of the island's bigger acacia trees he knew what he was going to do about it.

He stopped for a drink at a regular trickle on the cliff-face, took his knife and launched Sunbird for the second time today.

He paddled Sunbird to the spot where he thought he had seen Red Shark, threw over his light grapnel-anchor and followed it down for four metres. He found the box on the third dive, but he could not bring it up. He could lift it with effort, but he could not swim at all with the weight. He surfaced and panted for five minutes.

Ah, it's not worth it. About time for lunch anyway.

Lew pulled up the grapnel. And ran his thumb over the haft as he thought.

Ah, you can't let an old tin box beat you, can you?

Lew wrinkled his nose and threw the grapnel nearer the box. He dived again, caught two of the grapnel's flukes in one of the box's handles and returned to Sunbird.

He almost capsized Sunbird in the effort of bringing up the box but in a final heave he got it on to the deck. It was scarred and ugly, looking like a grey metal schoolcase with two leather handles, one pulled long and twisted. It was iron and was locked, padlocked, with something like a small transistor strapped on and protected in black rubber.

How d'you open it? Lew ran his hands over the edges of the box and frowned.

You've got a little of Max in you, after all.

Lew whipped his hands from the box as if it was hot.

Oh, come on! This is not theft. Why do you have to keep on thinking about him, all the time? Never Mick, Cindy or Leon, always Max. And he's dead and what's the good of it all?

So Lew lay back on the deck and thought of Cindy, just to push Max from his head. Blonde and freckled as if she'd walked into a spray-gun, very good at twitching her nose. And she could use her deafness as a positive advantage. If she couldn't work out what someone was saying to her she smiled and nodded as if whatever was said was so silly it didn't need an answer anyway. And when old Jackson tells everyone in the school assembly to stop that blasted talking she gossips away with her fingers under his nose. Never serious, except when she's worrying about an injured seagull.

Or when seeing Max's telescope for sale in a Mackay pawnshop.

Lew sat up in disgust. You really can't win.

He snorted, pulled his knife and cut the transistor from its rubber sheath. The sheath rolled from the deck but he was too tired to dive after it.

Chase frogs, Max. We're not stealing the creeps' box and we just can't get into it. But why not give them a bit of trouble, eh?

Lew fiddled with the transistor for ten minutes, failed to make it do anything, shoved it into a pocket in his togs and forgot about it.

He paddled Sunbird into the little bay at the side of Cataran Bay and hauled the box into the nearest thing to a patch of rain forest the island could produce.

Lew hooked his back and staggered back to Sunbird on rickety legs, suddenly an ancient castaway. He winked at a curious heron on a rock.

Like Ben Gunn or someone says, them that hides can find. And them that finds can hide.

He cackled, rubbed his hands and paddled back to his camp.

11

Max

Lew was slowly taking the transistor thing apart with his knife for the tenth time when a wave of small shadows swept across the bay. He was sure that he would know what the box contained, if only he could work out the purpose of the transistor. But for two long days it had told him nothing and he was almost relieved when the birds came.

He lifted his eyes from the small round battery and watched about twenty sulphur-crested cockatoos settle in trees, bushes, even on patches of sand. The big birds flapped their wings at each other, opened their beaks wide, flared their combs and danced about as if they had dropped from the sky for a brawl. Crusoe clicked his beak and flapped to the shelter of a stand of hoop pines.

They must be making a hell of a row, Lew thought.

He folded a piece of cloth over the transistor, put it back in his pocket, and tried to think of the sounds a flock of cockatoos would make. Harsh, like a lot of angry birds being strangled. Something like that.

Lew could still hear some sounds in his mind if he tried very hard—Mum singing an old song, a dog barking, a wave hissing up a beach—but you don't take in much when you are three. It is hardly worth the effort to remember now. But up to the sickness, the meningitis that boiled through his head and body, Lew had been able to hear everything from a pet mouse to a thunderstorm. So now he could look at a cockatoo dancing about with its mouth open and maybe remember the sound it was making.

Of course if he hadn't heard a particular sound before the sickness, like a jet engine, an elephant or an eagle, he just couldn't remember it. It was as if the sound didn't exist.

But it didn't really matter, did it? Who wants to hear an eagle? You see an eagle, that's all. You look up and see it.

Lew propped himself on his elbows and watched the birds.

But we're all like that, the Flying Finger Mob, more or less. The deafness is there; there's nothing you can do about it so you forget about it. No big deal.

Except for Max.

Lew sighed.

All right, Max wasn't like the rest of the Mob. Couldn't be. He didn't have his folks behind him. They thought he was stupid, or something, and they wanted to keep him hidden. For Max it was a big deal. And in the end Max didn't even have us.

Lew started to shrug the thought off, as he always had before. But this time he stopped and stared at the sand slowly draining from his fist.

Maybe it was our fault. We could see something and his folks couldn't see anything at all. Maybe we could have stopped it. But we weren't looking and Max was always a drag.

Lew pictured Max Schulman's face in the sand, a fat-faced boy with square glasses, slick black hair, a nervous mouth and constantly shifting eyes. The only time he wasn't frightened about missing something was when he had his telescope and the Mob was following him instead of him following the Mob. But it couldn't last. Mick joined the football club, Cindy started creating monster games on her computer, good ol' Lew was sailing around the Whitsundays and Leon was discovering what he called the 'head kick' of heavy metal rock. Nobody wanted to see Max's stars any more.

So Max found himself new mates, and they didn't want to see Max's stars either. Nobody liked Max's new mates. They always wore dark glasses, seemed to be talking very slowly and spent half their time in a dream. They looked strangely at each other as if they were keeping a secret. At a meeting of the Mob, Leon warned Max to stay away from his new mates, but Max just started to stay away from the Mob. What could you have done?

Well, Mick tried. When Cindy saw the telescope in the pawn shop he went round to Mr Schulman's office and tried to warn him. Mr Schulman tugged at his moustache and said: 'Thank you and your friends for being concerned about Max, but I am quite sure there is nothing to worry about. You have helped him in the past but now he's conquering his—ah—minor handicap he naturally moves toward—uh—normal—friends. I'm sure he will continue to see you all sometimes.' Bang.

And then there was the party. The last chance.

Lew watched Max's face change, as the breeze changed the sand before him. The hair was long and dull, a ragged piece of fishnet; the face was pale and gaunt; the eyes flat.

Lew lifted his gaze to the squalling birds in the air.

Happy birthday Lew.

He could remember the party, the last time Max had joined the Flying Finger Mob as clearly as if it was happening now. And that was the way it was then, Max *and* the Mob, not Max *in* the Mob. He'd dropped in because his parents had dropped him at the door on their way to a theatre club meeting, not because he wanted to see his old friends. Now you had to watch what you said, otherwise he'd think you were getting at him, and he wasn't interested in anything you were doing—not any more.

But he was at the Mob's party, watching Cindy telling rude jokes with her fingers and funny face, walking about, saying a few words to Mum, walking in the empty rooms in the house, drinking lemonade behind Leon, and walking off into the shadows again. So you followed him to pull him into the centre of the party, to stop him from feeling alone.

And you saw him put Mum's old figurine in his bag and walk on. You started to rush forward, to grab him, but Mick caught you by the shoulder and stopped you. 'Just wait a little,' Mick's fingers said. 'He used to be a friend.' So a little later Mick came up behind Max and lifted the figurine from his bag. 'I guess he needs money real bad.' Mick said silently as he passed the figurine back.

And that was it. You never saw Max again. And what could you do? Cindy tried, Mick tried, you tried. It didn't do any good. Maybe you should have got him out to the island. Maybe. But it was too late.

Lew threw a pebble at two of the fighting birds and felt the transistor thump his chest.

Look, it's no good. Leave Max with the cockatoos. Get out and go visit an eagle.

12

Eagle's Nest

Half an hour later Lew walked from his camp with a small shoulder bag slapping his hip. He walked along the beach and into the straggly bush, scattering three blustering cockatoos as he began climbing. This time he could feel the wind sighing down the slope before he cleared the lower bushes, and he expected to be blown flat before he reached Mosstrooper.

He thought of Max at the beginning of the climb but the boy seemed to fade away with the cockatoos and he could feel the transistor thing with every step he took. He gladly returned to the painless mystery of the box.

In the two days he had been left alone on the island with the box he had been drawn back to it a few times. He had attempted to open it twice with a heavy branch, his knife and a tin opener but had succeeded only in breaking the tin opener. He had thought of building a fire under it, but he couldn't see what good that would do, and it could even damage his island. In the end he had left it alone, and just tried to work out what the transistor was for. He had hunted for oysters round the rim of Mosstrooper, dived in the north deeps of the bay, photographed peculiar ferns, and thought about it all the time.

Lew straightened as the slope eased and was forced to step back. The warm air was scudding over the grass, heaving against his chest, streaking his hair. He opened his mouth, let his cheeks flap a little and laughed. He walked quickly to the spread of the saddle to see low waves exploding on the rock tongue below, curling over the rock, sliding away. He looked up and four ospreys were riding the air like kites. There would be eagles up there too.

A great day for climbing. If you don't get blown off.

Lew walked easily along the saddle and up through the brittle brush and the blackbows—tall grass clumps growing around single stemmed seed pods, like spears. He reached the small forest of thin casuarinas and hoop pines which formed a ragged beard for the granite face of Mosstrooper's grim soldier.

Now for a little work, if you please.

He had climbed the peak so many times he was beginning to form a path, but only for his eyes. He worked up and through the forest, pulling himself from trunk to trunk as the wind swayed and shook the trees above his head.

The box looked something like a treasure chest, didn't it? Well, a little bit.

He was through the forest and under the soldier's nose. He worked sideways past some low overgrown caves into a curling gust from the sea below. He stopped until the wind steadied and then moved on very slowly. He had explored many of the caves in a search for paintings and spearheads left by the aborigines before they had been driven from the islands, but there had been nothing yet. He would look at other caves later.

73

Theo and Col had probably snagged the box on a fishing line and didn't want anyone to know what they had found until they had had a look at it themselves.

Lew put his right arm through the bag's strap to settle the bag low on his back and used both hands to haul himself along the rain-stained cliff of the soldier's cheek. He was higher than hoop pines now and the low brush was giving way to stark rock.

Maybe they were worried that the government would want a piece of the box, so they had dropped it off before being rescued. That figured.

Lew flexed his fingers and climbed carefully along a seam on the soldier's forehead. He had almost fallen around here, almost tumbled over a granite face to the trees, and he had spent an hour grimly imagining what he would do on a remote part of his lonely island with a broken leg. Now he climbed very slowly, testing the force of the wind with his body before he reached up, found a handhold and heaved. It took him almost half an hour to reach the flattened scrub of the soldier's hairline, but after the granite face he could almost stroll to the summit of Mosstrooper, 228 metres from the sea.

Just before he reached the peak he stepped a little to the left and spotted Joe's nest, a tumbled fortress of sticks and brown leaves two metres across, balanced on a ledge high over the surging waves. Lew stretched out in an effort to see if there were any eggs in the nest, but a larger eagle than Joe swooped out of the sky and stopped in the air near the nest.

'Josie!' Lew shouted in delight at the great brown and white bird.

The sea eagle lay motionless in the wind as several

wing feathers were lifted and combed by a gust. It kept watching Lew.

'Sorry,' said Lew and moved away.

The eagle lifted the edge of a wing and soared effortlessly to rejoin its mate circling the sun.

Lew had found the nest of Joe and Josie two years ago, but he had never tried to reach it. He considered that impolite, apart from being downright dangerous, but a little curiosity never hurt anybody if you could get away with it. Did it?

But you still can't open the box.

Lew hauled himself over a whitened branch and stepped out on the summit of Mosstrooper. A stride, a small jump and he had reached the flat rock he called the Throne. He slowly looked about him and the thrill was still there.

Settle yourself on the Throne and you are sitting on top of the world. Look west, beyond tiny Doloraine Island, and you can almost see the flat pattern of the Great Barrier Reef on the curve of the horizon. Turn and the slumbering lizard of Border Island lies beneath you, the bay, the spine of the hills stretching south, a strange arrow of piled rocks, and the two islets snuggling up to the island like baby lizards. Beyond the hills of the island lie the pure white rim of Whitehaven Beach on Whitsunday Island, the crescents of Hill Inlet's shifting sand and the sombre green mountains of Hook Island . . .

Mum would love it here. She'd set up her easel, her canvas, squirt her oils, and get it all down. She'd forget about the boredom of painting other people's signs . . .

A crawling speck in the sky caught the corner of Lew's eye.

A small seaplane was approaching the island from

the Barrier Reef and it reminded Lew of something. He thought a minute then shrugged it aside.

No, Mum wouldn't ever get here. She just couldn't make the climb. It's the Mob that should be here after all. Of course Cindy would complain every step of the way, but she'd love the view. And they'd all get together to solve his problem. They would work out what was in the box in nothing flat, open it in an hour.

Lew smiled and pulled the transistor thing from his pocket and spread the cloth on the Throne.

'What d'you say, Mick?' Lew said with his hands and voice to the patch of sky containing the plane.

'You don't know? You're not much good, are you? Don't hit, don't hit! What's that Cindy? It's just a simple battery-powered transistor? With maybe a micro-chip? But what does it do?'

The seaplane purred past Mosstrooper, not all that much higher and close enough for him to see the blur of the single propeller before the cockpit. Lew waved at it. There was something . . .

'Where was the box found, Leon? Way out on the reef, where that plane's coming from. It must have come from a wreck. There's many wrecks out there that nobody knows—' Lew stopped.

Except the box was not old. It was not encrusted with barnacles and coral. It was not even marked with rust. It was new, so new it might as well have been dumped in the water overnight.

'Ah, beat it, Max.' Lew waved at the air and concentrated on the shrinking seaplane. It was the smallest of Air Whitsunday's fleet returning with no more than three tourists from the Reef. Out on the Reef it would land on its belly then lean on the small floats on the wings. It liked being kicked into the air by a small wave on take-off. Now it was passing between Whit-sunday and Hook Islands on the way home.

Lew closed his eyes tiredly. 'Go haunt somebody else's island, Max. What d'you want?'

Oh.

There had been a plane coming from beyond the islands that early morning when Col had rolled that gas cylinder. Remember? A light, private plane, not a seaplane. What would a plane like that be doing over the Reef before sunrise?

The transistor. It is a radio transmitter.

Lew stared at the transmitter and backed away from it, as if it was alive. The joke he had been playing on Col and Theo had gone terribly wrong. He had to put the box where he had found it while he still could.

He snatched up the transistor, rolled from the Throne and started climbing hastily back down Mosstrooper.

As Red Shark creamed into Cataran Bay below him.

13

The Wrecker

Col stood on the bow of Red Shark and swept the radio direction finder across Cataran Bay. 'No,' he said finally. 'Not a peep.'

'No worries.' Theo slowed the boat until the bow wave became a ripple. 'Batteries could be dead, or drowned. We don't need it now.'

'Okay.' Col pushed the aerial into the box, threw the box to his seat and picked up the anchor.

'A minute.' Theo was trying to line up a tree near the beach with an odd-shaped clump on the saddle as well as a leaning hoop pine high on Mosstrooper with a slab of rock that slid into the bay. He was finding it as difficult as balancing three balls on his nose.

'Stinking birds.' Col scratched his maroon togs and glared at the shrieking cockatoos milling round the beach. 'Shut up!' he yelled, and was ignored.

'Ah, that'll do.' Theo waved a finger at Col and Col cut the motor.

Col threw out the anchor and went with it, allowing it to pull him down to the shallow reef. He had left his tank and flippers in the boat because this dive did not need them. He expected to be down for thirty seconds and back on board with the box in under a minute.

Two minutes later he burst the surface, gasping.

'Got it?' Theo said.

Col shook his head.

'What's your trouble?' Theo sounded a little worried.

Col gulped in air. 'It's not down there.'

'I really do have to do everything, don't I? Course it's down there. Go back and find it.'

Col raised a defiant thumb but breathed deeply and duck-dived. He's as bad as Aunt Emma, Col thought as he kicked angrily over the coral. They're all the same. 'Call that floor swept? I'll sweep it myself.' 'You mean that's *all* the homework you've done, Starkey?' 'You're not going out with those painted louts again?' and on, and on and on. The hell with it!

Col returned empty-handed again and hauled himself back into the boat.

'What's the matter with you?' Theo roared. 'Can't you find anything that doesn't flash at you?'

'It's you. You've just got your markers screwed up.' Col reached for his tank.

'Don't get cocky with me, boy. I don't screw up *anything*. Ever.'

'So where's the box? It's not down there.'

'It's got to be.' Theo blinked. For a moment he sounded uncertain.

'Yeah. But not down here. I've got to look for it, haven't I?'

'You'd just better find it, that's all.'

'I'm going to find it. With none of your smart navigation tricks.' Col slipped on his flippers, adjusted his tank and fell backwards from Red Shark.

He remained under water for more than half an hour, criss-crossing the bay constantly, marking his progress with a trail of bursting air bubbles. Theo watched the bubbles from the back of the boat, crouched in a tight hunch. As time went on he balled his hands and slowly pounded the hull.

Col surfaced with something black dangling from his fingers.

'You find it?' Theo was strangely breathless.

'This mean something to you?' Col felt a strange satisfaction as he threw the black object to Theo.

Theo caught the object, fingered it and frowned. Then he looked up with the beginnings of a smile. 'It's the casing of the radio transmitter. You found it . . .' He caught the expression on Col's face.

'That's all there is. I looked all round.'

'Ah, you're . . . you're useless. It's got to be there.' Theo rubbed his fist white.

Col started to unload himself. 'Some greasy parrot's pinched it.' Ten minutes ago Col had realized the box had been taken and had got rid of some of his anger and bitterness under water. Now at least he had the rare opportunity of passing on the pain.

He heaved the tank into the boat and followed it with a kick and a roll. He was almost smiling.

'D'you know what the Big Man's going to do to you? Eh?' Theo jabbed Col hard in the stomach with a podgy finger. His voice had become high-pitched and unsteady.

Col looked uncertain. 'Me? Why me? You're the boss. You get all the money; you get all the blame.'

'You know how he's going to take it? Do you? He's not going to believe this. You saw how he was when we went in the first time without the box. He's going to reckon we pinched the box ourselves and that's going to be it.' He punched his palm.

Col sat up and the touch of glee died on his face. 'What'll we do?' he said.

'And maybe he's not so wrong.' Theo was regaining control of his voice.

'What?'

'How do I know you didn't come out here by yourself and lift the box yesterday? Eh?'

'I wouldn't do that, Theo. You know that.'

'Oh, I do, do I? Or perhaps you found it down there and hid it so you could pick it up later. Maybe that's what I'll tell the Big Man.'

'You can't do that . . .' Col's voice was fading to a whisper when he saw a flash of yellow near the beach. 'Maybe he's still here.'

'Who?'

But Col was in the water, scything toward a small finger of the bay. By the time Theo had started the motor Col had kicked off his flippers and was splashing past a rain-hollowed boulder. He stopped, looked about him and hauled a yellow-hulled catamaran on to the beach.

Theo started the motor, hauled in the anchor and followed Col in. 'Who is it?' he called.

'Dunno.' Col hauled up the mainsail and nodded at the sun and the bird painted on the dacron. 'It's the Clown.'

Theo walked across to the catamaran and kicked one of the hulls. Then he shook his head. 'Shouldna done that. He's probably watching. Get the boat in the water, where he can see it.'

Col walked the cat into the water and towed it to face the centre of the beach. He did not know why, but he did not like the cat at all.

'Call him.'

'Sure. Hey, Deadhead!'

'You great nit! We want to bring him down to us, not send him off hiding in the hills.'

'Doesn't matter. He's deaf. Can't hear a thing.'

'Oh. Oh yeah. Okay, he's still got eyes.' Theo turned to Mosstrooper, smiling like a quiz show compère and beckoning with his entire arm. 'Come down, Stupid, you dear boy—what's the little sneak's name?'

'Lew Thomas.' Now Col knew exactly why he disliked the boat almost as much as the boy. Lew Thomas, son of Mr and Mrs Thomas, who lived together at home. And Mr Thomas had given—*given!* the boat to the kid so he could make the Whitsundays his playground, and Mrs Thomas had even painted his sails. He was given it all on a plate.

'Come on down, Mister Lew,' Theo was saying quietly, smiling up at the saddle. 'We won't hurt you— much—and we're going to give you a beautiful toffee apple when we see you. Come on and tell us what a smart boy you have been with our box. He can speak, can't he?'

'Sort of. Hard to understand.'

'It'll do. Can you see him?'

Both Theo and Col scanned the hills, but nothing was moving apart from the cockatoos.

'All right. Get the axe,' said Theo.

Col pushed the catamaran toward the beach, its main swinging idly, then jogged over to Red Shark. He pulled the hatchet from a bag under the seat and came back to the cat.

'Push the boat into deeper water, okay?' said Theo, still smiling at the hills.

Col turned the cat and towed it to waist-deep water. The main caught a touch of wind and the cat moved away from Col and his hatchet, almost as if it were trying to escape. Col caught it easily by the rudder.

'Show the boy the axe.' The smile disappeared.

Col waved the hatchet, looked at the painted sun and thought about his own mother. He had liked Laura a lot, even with her boyfriends. Oh sure, they had brawled. Who doesn't? But she was all right when she wasn't in a hurry, or worried about money. She would talk to you, like you weren't a kid any more. But she upped and left when the Clown dropped him in it. As if it was the last straw. One morning she's there, then bang, she's gone.

'No sign of him,' said Theo. 'All right, hit the boat.'

Col hesitated and struck the starboard rudder with the flat of the hatchet.

Nothing moved.

Like Dad. Bang, and gone somewhere in Western Australia. Couldn't remember his face now. Couldn't remember anything about him. Well what d'you expect? What does a three-year-old ankle biter remember?

'Hit it again.'

But she should have stayed. She didn't give you a chance, no chance at all.

Col drove the blade into the starboard hull, twisted it and jerked it out.

Just because of the Clown's nose and Jackson's mouth. I stuck up for you all the time Laura, against your lousy sister Emma—Jackson, Theo, all of them. But you wouldn't stick with me. You had to run.

Col watched the water rush into the gash he had made and hit it again and again, driving the blade deep into the fibreglass and twisting it so the boat groaned as he pulled it out. He panted for a moment, then

83

jerked the cat round to attack the other hull, the mast swaying over his head.

'Col . . .'

The boom swung lightly against his head and he ripped his hatchet through the bird and the sun.

'No!' A faint and desperate cry.

A small figure standing high on the saddle.

'There he is!' Theo shouted. 'Get him, Col!'

14

Hunt

Lew stood stark on a wind-scored rock with his right arm stretching toward Cataran Bay and his mouth wide. He was gasping, choking, as Sunbird heeled in the water, the sail torn apart and flapping.

Then he realized what he had done.

Fat Theo was standing on the beach pointing up at him. Col had let Sunbird go and was leaping toward the beach, each step exploding a circle of water behind the jerking hatchet. He grabbed something from Red Shark, but he hardly lost a step and bolted across the grass as if he were trying to take off.

Lew let his arm sag to his side and stepped quite slowly from the rock.

He didn't think he was frightened. He had watched Col and Theo finish their search of the bay with a calm patience, and when Col had found Sunbird he had felt disappointment more than alarm. He had even thought of standing up and pointing out the hiding place of the box when Col was waving for him to show himself. But that was before he had remembered Max again. He had been thrust on to his feet by the shock of the destruction of Sunbird but the shock had somehow passed. Now he didn't know if what he felt was fear, fury or grief.

But his feet had decided for him.

He looked down in surprise to see his legs pounding the rocky earth, pushing him across the curve of the saddle. His legs were jogging, but he had not told them to do anything at all. At least he didn't think so.

Then he realized that Col was leaping up the slope behind him with a swinging hatchet and he had gone berserk. In less than three strides Lew's wandering jog became a headlong rush. His feet flew through the clumps of grass, finding flat rocks and thrusting him up the dying slope. His bag was slamming his leg.

This is not real. It can't be real.

But he was still accelerating when he reached the crest of the saddle. For a few moments panic hurled him across the flat so fast his legs were running far behind his body, the wind was battering his face, grass spears were breaking over his arms and stomach like surf. So fast he couldn't feel frightened, couldn't stop, couldn't even think.

Lew crossed the flat of the saddle in less than five seconds, but the ground began to slope away from him. He took a great stride over a leaning bush, saw the earth far beneath him and began to retract his foot as he fell, the bag hitting him on the ear.

He stabbed at a blackbow, skidded on a fern and rolled toward a distant table of dark rock ringed by exploding waves. He tumbled helplessly for several moments, then clutched at a clump of bracken, pounded a sliding rock with his foot and stopped. He bit a strand of grass and watched a tumble of pebbles, rocks and loose gravel bounce past his feet, career down the slope and leap a washed cliff to splatter on the table rock.

That was nearly it, wasn't it? What have you got yourself into? All right, take it easy. Work it out later.

He looked up at the tough calm of Mosstrooper and considered the low caves round the beard.

Hide there and they'll never find you.

Lew slipped off the bag, thrust it behind a bush and drew himself into a crouch.

But how do you get there from here? Go back to the saddle and Col would see you. How close to the saddle is he now?

Lew could still see Col driving his hatchet into Sunbird, again and again . . .

No, you've got to go down to hide, away from him. Always away.

Lew got to his feet, crept over a broad mass of flat black rock and skittered through tangled grass toward the table rock. The hair on the back of his neck had begun to prickle and he wanted to run again, but he knew he could not. He skirted the cliff framing the table rock, constantly looking back at the saddle, constantly trying to pick a hiding place.

Climb down to the rock and you can hide at the foot of the cliffs, even on the rock itself.

Lew stood near a hoop pine with a sloping gully before him and waves seething past at the bottom.

Now? No, no. Get down there and there's nowhere you can go. You are cut off, like swimming into a net.

Lew glimpsed a movement back on the saddle and crouched, feeling as conspicuous as a six storey hotel. Col was up on top and looking, but he hadn't seen him yet. The crouch became a slow crawl to the hoop pine, only standing when he was able to put the trunk between him and the saddle. He backed slowly away down the slope, watching the trunk and the skyline until he reached another stand of pines fringing the sea cliffs.

He saw the silhouette of a man separating from a bush on the saddle and moving toward Mosstrooper.

Lew dug his nails into the rough bark and forced himself to stay motionless.

Keep going. All the way up the Peak.

The man stopped.

No, really, I'm up there. Can't you see me in one of the caves? Go on, find me where I'm not.

But the man turned back and joined another, thicker, man carrying a stick and some kind of box. They looked about them, then the thicker man waved the box at Mosstrooper and opened his mouth.

Fat Theo's shouting, isn't he? Sorry, I'm not listening.

Lew pushed a quick giggle into his nose and sneezed.

Don't be silly. This is serious.

Then Fat Theo pointed the box downhill and both men started to move toward Lew.

The transmitter!

Lew's right hand snaked to his pocket, pulled the wrapped transistor clear and pitched it low toward the table rock, as if it were a bomb. He had moved so fast he hardly felt the transistor between his fingers, only a faint rasping sensation on his thumb told him it had been there. But he knew he had been too slow.

Col was striding ahead of Theo, as if he knew exactly where he was going.

Of course he knows! With that transmitter in your pocket you might as well have been waving a flag from your hiding place. It was too late to throw it away. What do you do, run? There's nothing else.

Lew leant his head against the tree and scored the

bark with his nails. Something cold and fierce was shaking him like a puppy with a rag doll. His right foot jerked from behind the tree and cocked itself for flight.

No.

Move, but move slowly so they don't see you. You've got a bit of time before Col gets here and they still can't see you. Just take it easy.

Lew eased through the trees, skirting the cliff and moving away from the table rock. Theo seemed to be shouting at Col, waving away from Lew and toward the table rock. Col turned for a moment but kept on moving straight up the slope. Theo followed him half way, then stopped, thought and climbed back a little.

He's watching for any movement, Lew thought.

Lew slowed his retreat to a slow slither but he could see Col's face very clearly now, glowing with anger. He was swinging the hatchet with every step and Lew wanted desperately to bolt.

Maybe you can still tell them where the box is and they'll leave you alone.

Col was no more than twenty metres away now.

If they'd come an hour later, just an hour, it would've been all right. The box would've been back where it was dumped, they would've picked it up and gone. Sunbird would be all right. I would be all right. I don't want their lousy box . . .

Col stooped and lifted Lew's bag. He sniffed at it like a suspicious dog, searched through it and hurled it to the sea. He stopped by the gully leading to the table rock and jerked his head about.

That's what he'll do if he catches you. Don't give him a chance.

Col took a step and stopped moving.

89

He's listening. Can he hear me breathing? Am I making sounds he can hear, rolling pebbles, pushing grass? How do I stop the sound? How do I know?

Col turned to the gully and clambered down to the table rock. Lew allowed himself a moment of relief and watched his right hand shake.

That bad? he thought. That bad. What have you got yourself into?

Lew made a fist and the shaking stopped.

Well, Col and Theo are criminals, heavies, the lot. We're not kidding any more.

Ah, come on . . .

You want to come up with a funny story about the box? Or Sunbird? Or what they are doing now?

Okay, okay.

Lew began to crawl from the pines to some ragged palms to his right. Within a few minutes Col would come up the gully again and start searching toward him. He must move fast while he could, but he must not be seen by Theo. He looked back at his legs, making sure he wasn't dislodging stones or snapping twigs, and he kept his head way down.

But how bad are they? Col was in school just a year ago, in the next building.

A clump of needle grass came away in Lew's hand.

Watch it! That box is nothing but bad. So bad they have to dump it in the Reef from a plane at night, and sneak it ashore by boat. So bad they dump it here and sail out into the open sea in a sinking boat so they won't be caught with it. So valuable they don't dump it out there, where they get into trouble, and call for help. No, they come all the way here to get it safe before getting themselves safe somewhere else.

You don't *know* that . . .

So they are smugglers or something. Big-time smugglers, or maybe little-time smugglers working for a big-time boss. Doesn't matter which. They have to get the box. They just can't go home without it. And they can't get the box without you. Beauty, mate, you've really done it now.

Lew closed his eyes for a moment. Then he looked up at the sky and already the sun was disappearing behind the lizard hump of the island.

Theo strolled near the saddle, tucking his long stick under his arm.

Hey, come on. They are still looking for that transmitter, not you, and if they don't see you in the next two hours the sun will be gone and they'll never catch you.

Lew watched Theo for a few seconds and decided to keep moving toward him.

It's like chess. Keep thinking it's a game like chess. Theo is not as dangerous as Col, so keep away from Col. If you keep climbing near the saddle Col will have to search an area which is getting bigger every minute. Col won't get near Theo and if Theo sees you, just run free. You can race Fat Theo on one leg. See, it's not so bad.

Col hauled himself out of the gully and shouted something at Theo. Theo shouted back and threw the box away. He pointed his stick at the hoop pines, but Col propped his arms on his knees and panted before blundering toward the pines.

They're getting tired. Just keep going.

Lew pulled himself over some jagged rocks with Col below and Theo above him. Briefly Col and Theo seemed to converge on him but Theo turned away toward Mosstrooper and Col stayed on the cliff edge.

Then Lew felt a heavy twig snap beneath him. He stopped, wondering how loud the sound had been.

Col continued to hunt from the pines to the palms but Theo looked up and pointed his stick in Lew's general direction. Two blackbows snapped and long grass shivered.

He's got a gun!

Lew slid under a low bush and forced himself to be still.

Col and Theo shouted at each other then Theo walked near to Lew. Lew saw Theo's feet through the grass and the brush, coming, coming, and standing still.

Don't move, don't breathe, don't look. You're caught, you're caught . . .

But when Lew's eyes flickered open again the feet were going away.

Lew lay still for five minutes while he eased his nails from the trenches they had made in his palms. He climbed the hill past the saddle slowly, until he could look down on the searching men. Then he stopped.

The sun was gone now. Deep shadows were creeping over the island and the first handful of stars had appeared over the peak. Theo and Col were still trudging over the eastern slope, still shouting at each other, but they would never find him now. Lew sagged on his elbows as the afternoon's terror dripped slowly from him.

That's that, he thought, and dropped a limp leg on a clump of grass. Now he was very tired, weak and with a thousand aches and cuts throbbing across his body, but he had survived. He even tried a feeble smile.

After a while he rolled over and looked at the still

silver of Cataran Bay. And saw the wreckage of Sunbird drifting slowly out of the bay.

There wasn't much left to see now. The mast was almost parallel with the water and only one hull was visible, rearing from the water. The months of work he and Dad had done in changing a scarred and mouldy wreck into a slick sailing machine had been reduced to a sausage on a stick. And Mum's sail, the wandering gull and the warm sun, was now just a rag trailing in the moonlight.

Lew turned away.

'Okay,' he said. 'Okay.' And he began to feel angry.

15

Night

Col stumbled over a hidden root and swore. 'Can't see him now! Can't see *anything* now. This is a waste of time.'

'Come here and shut up.' Theo was a silhouette on the saddle, a gleam of the moon on his shoulder, the glow of a cigarette in his mouth.

Col trudged up to Theo, slashing tiredly at the blackbows with his hatchet. 'It's no good. He could be just about anywhere now.'

'Look, shut up. We've been doing this all wrong. We can still catch him.'

'We got a month, maybe?'

'We've been looking for him, right?'

'Yeah, so?'

'No, wrong. We shoulda been listening for him instead.'

'Eh?'

'He's deaf, isn't he? He never knows what sound he makes. Just go over to the mountain and just sit and listen for a while. The baby boy might stumble into your arms.'

'This is stupid.'

'Just do it, right?'

Col kicked his way to a flat hunk of granite and sat. He could see the white crescents of breaking waves at the table rock but there was no force in their sound. The wind had dropped and the steady flow and ebb of the sea was little more than a soft surge of the breeze. There was nothing to listen to.

He took off his right sandshoe carefully and winced as the slash on his instep came away from the cotton. He had snatched the sandshoes from Red Shark as he ran after the kid but he had not put them on until the grass and rocks tore at his feet. The kid had caused him a great deal of pain today—all that crawling over the coral in the bay as well, all that running and searching through the scrub in his bare legs—oh, the kid was going to get it.

Col put his sandshoe back on and listened again, carefully now. He could hear the flap of a tired bird from the trees near the bay below him, the whirr of a dragonfly behind his ear and the soft clatter of leaves from a bush, but he could not hear any sound that could be made by an animal or a boy.

He frowned. They should have caught the kid by now. Stupid kid, couldn't understand half of what you said to him and he got his words all wrong. But he got here on that playboat and he pinched the box and he can't be caught. Maybe he's a little brighter than Aunt Emma after all. Yeah, yeah, a roast chicken is brighter than Emma. Once she even thought her milk money was being pinched because she'd forgotten where she'd hidden it. Silly berk.

Anyway, the kid shouldna been on this stinking island. His old man shouldna let him this far out. And what about his old woman? Don't they know it's

95

dangerous out here? Anyway, what does he want with the box? Playing games? Well, we're not playing, kid.

Col hunched forward and scratched a knuckle. He thought bleakly about losing the Chrysler and worse, about what he would have to do if Lew was not caught, if the box was not recovered.

You'd leave Theo, for a start. Let him face the Big Man on his own. Go west. If Pops can hide for thirteen years over there you can do it too. But the cops would be after you; the Big Man would be after you, all the time. The kid just can't do that to you . . .

Col slapped at the high whine of a mosquito. He pushed himself from his rock and returned to Theo.

'Nothing?' Theo said.

'No. They're eating me.'

'Mmn?'

'Mossies.'

'That all you're worried about?'

'Maybe we'd better check the boat.'

Theo looked up in sudden alarm. 'We've—' He lurched toward the path to the bay but slowed down for the second step and the second word, '—ah—well, we're not doing any good up here now, anyway. We might as well go down. You go down first and get a fire going.'

Col started at an easy pace but accelerated until he was almost running down the steepest part of the slope. He had imagined being stuck on the island with no food or water, waiting with the box for the police—without knowing where the box was.

But Red Shark was sitting on the wet sand, left by the receding tide. He started to build a fire but remembered the boy's camping equipment. When Theo puffed on to the beach the billy was boiling on the gas stove and Col was examining the tins.

'The kid looked after himself, y'know,' Col said. 'Tea?'

'Yeah. Got an idea.'

Theo sat on the sand and smiled.

An hour later Col pushed Red Shark into the water, turned it and clambered in as Theo started the motor. The boat roared out of the bay and turned toward Hook Island.

16

Marooned

Lew watched the men on the beach in a drowsy effort to stay awake. He saw the long shadow of Col run out on the pale sand, check the ugly boat, and wander about uncertainly before he got something from Lew's camp site. He saw the glimmer of a spark in Col's hand as he crouched, then a low glow at his feet.

He's making tea, Lew thought. With my stuff. So what's new?

Theo joined Col and they looked back at the saddle, the moon catching their faces.

Well, can you see me, eh? Go on, enjoy my tea. It's all you'll ever get.

They squatted on the sand for a while, then walked about the beach for a few minutes and Col humped the boat into the water. Theo threw something large into the boat, heaved himself aboard and started the motor.

Lew sat up abruptly. They're leaving. No, they've found the box. No, they haven't moved from the beach. What?

Col swung into the boat. Theo revved the motor several times, as if he wanted to waken every bird and insect on the island, then headed for the open sea.

They've worked out where the box is. No, they're

going past the little bay. They are going, really going. Why?

Lew watched the boat turn toward Hook Island past the point and stood, frowning. He brushed grass and green ants from his arms and legs and scratched his ribs.

Why is because they know they can't catch me and they can't find the box without me. They've gone so they can hide when Sergeant Austin comes.

Lew walked easily down to the saddle but hesitated at the path down to the bay.

Better not. Wait until the morning. They just might come back.

He looked for a fairly flat patch of earth and lay down, ignoring the pebbles, mosquitoes and crawling insects. And slept.

★ ★ ★

Next morning there was no sign of Red Shark. Lew staggered to his feet, ran his tongue around a dry mouth, rubbed life into painfully dented arms and climbed down to the bay. He was going to have a strong cup of tea with a long squirt of condensed milk, and kippers with onions and maybe some chips. After all, he had missed dinner last night.

Except there was nothing left at all.

His camp site was now nothing more than a trampled slope of grass and sand. The tent had been torn from its pegs, the tins scooped from their hollow in the sand, the vegetables taken in their net bags. No knives, forks, plates, mugs, frypan, stove—not even a match.

So that was it.

Lew sat heavily in the sand. Crusoe sat on a nearby rock and waited.

All simple, isn't it? Take all the food and everything and go back to Airlie Beach. Maybe come back a few days later and there's Lew on the beach with his tongue hanging out and he'll tell you where the box is for a slice of bread and a mouthful of water . . .

Lew looked about him, at the holes left by the pegs, the deep circle left by the stove, the straight trench running into the still water of Sunbird's harbour.

They have taken everything.

Lew shrugged at the crow and opened his hands.

Crusoe turned and flew away.

You might as well. Sorry.

Lew ran his fingers along the trench, stopped and looked at his hand.

Good plan, but it doesn't work, does it?

Lew got up, walked down to the beginning of the path to the saddle and pressed through the undergrowth to the trickle of water down the orchard cliff. He pressed his face against the rock, using his tongue to channel the water into his mouth. After five minutes he stepped back, cupped his hands under the trickle and washed his face.

That's a start. Now what do we have for breakfast and lunch?

He walked away from the cliff to the flattened spot under a tree where the occasional visitor always pitched his tent. He could see the faint trenches that would keep water from flooding under the tent, and he scattered the mouldy leaves outside the trenches with slow patience. Eventually his fingers found a stained tent peg, threw it in the air and caught it. He walked back to the beach, considered removing his sandshoes, decided against it and swam from the beach with the peg rammed into his shorts.

He reached the oyster rocks after a leisurely fifteen minute swim and removed his shirt to spread across a black rock above the tide-line. He rested in the sun for a while, watching the empty sea between Border Island and Hook Island, then dived for his dinner.

The oysters crowded each other on a gently sloping rock face with small fish darting between forests of tall seaweed. Lew set his feet apart on the wrinkled black shells and used the peg to prise an oyster slowly from the rock. He swam to the surface for a little pant and put the shell on his shirt. He brought up five more and then stopped for a late breakfast.

But opening the shells was harder than getting them. The peg was too blunt to insert between the two shells and after struggling for almost half an hour Lew gave up and bashed the shell with a rock. He had to pick shell slivers from the meat, but it was still a delicious meal.

He was leaning back on his rock as Joe fell from the sky.

They've shot him! he thought, and leapt up in horror. Then smiled and relaxed. The eagle was not falling, but plummeting for something near the oyster rocks. The wings were folded back, turning the hunting bird into a missile with a hooked beak and a cocked claw. Joe seemed just to slap the water before stretching his wings and climbing, a large fish in his claws.

Wanna swap? Lew thought. Nah, skip it. Nice of you to visit. Like yesterday's show?

Joe disappeared round Mosstrooper and Lew looked for more oysters. He collected ten more, bagged them with his shirt and kicked his way easily back across the bay. He was looking up into a perfect blue dome with the eagles and the ospreys circling the glinting peak and for a while he almost forgot Theo, Col and the box. Then he wondered where Sunbird had finally sunk.

Wish I could see what you see, he thought. Okay, Sunbird, Theo and Col, that's for later. Food is the important thing now. You could keep getting oysters but you'd get sick of them. What about fish? Rub hard rock over the end of the peg to sharpen it, tie it to a straight branch with a bit of vine and you have a spear.

Lew stopped kicking.

But you have to hunt in the shallows. Here. In the bay, in the sanctuary. You promised no fishing in the bay, but you can't fish anywhere else. Well, what're you going to do?

Lew started kicking again.

Of course you're going to hunt in the shallows. You've got to eat. The sanctuary is suspended. 'Course you still have to hit the beasties.

Lew kicked an outcrop of coral and sat up. He lugged the swollen shirt to the beach, spread it on the sand and examined the point of the peg.

Crusoe landed two metres away.

Fair weather bird, Lew thought. But he smashed an oyster shell and threw half the oyster to the crow.

But you have to eat the fish raw.

Lew's nose wrinkled.

Who said? You only have to swim out to where the yachts anchor and you've got all the broken bottles you want. A piece of curved glass can act like a magnifying glass. Get it to concentrate the sun on some dry leaves and you've got a fire. Shove the fish on a green stick and grill it. Lovely.

Crusoe picked delicately at the oyster.

Lew picked a large oval pebble from the sand and started scraping the point of the peg across it.

Sergeant Austin doesn't have to get here in a hurry. He can take a month. Just so he catches the wreckers in the end. Hey, you're starting to foam at the mouth over Sunbird. What about Max?

Come on, what about Max? He has got nothing to do with this. He's a weird little creep, he's a thief and he's dead. Stay mad over Sunbird.

Lew felt the bright point on the peg and sucked his thumb.

Except he wasn't always a creep and a thief. Once he knew every mountain on the moon like they were in his backyard, knew about quasars, black holes and quarks. Our neighbourhood spaceman. And then his new mates moved in, and what's the difference between them and Theo and Col? Nothing. Nothing at all . . .

Lew turned the peg in his hands and stared through it, until the point caught the sun and he blinked.

Hey, hey, the water! Get a few of the cans you buried in the little bay and wash them in the sea, put them under the cliff with palm leaves as funnels for the water. Sorry, Theo, Col, but this marooning bit just isn't going to work. This is going to be fun.

Crusoe batted frantically into the air and scudded across the beach.

Lew looked up in curiosity.

Col was ten metres away and running at him.

17

Run

For an instant Lew stared at the hatchet in Col's hand, at the grin on his face and at the sand spraying from his leaping feet. Then he was moving, had moved, as instantly and as instinctively as a cricketer reaching for a fast catch. He rolled toward Col and to his right. Col's left foot caught him solidly on the shoulder, but Col was tipped into the sand.

What happened? he thought. It was his first thought and his body was still reacting by itself.

His knees and hands were crabbing under his chest as Col sprawled on the beach. Lew glimpsed Col tumbling away from him with his mouth open in anger as he tried to straighten his legs. One foot trembled and turned in the sand and his body seemed to be as heavy and immovable as a cow in a bog, and Col was kicking down hard and beginning to leap to his feet.

He's got me, he's got—

Then he was away with a gasp and a lurch, clawing at the air as his sandshoes made a squelching rhythm with his toes. He felt a faint touch of relief which died in two strides. He was bolting toward the base of the peak and the beach was going to stop in a ragged trail of rocks, boulders and a sheer stone wall in less than

104

twenty metres. He veered right and ploughed up a gully of silk-soft sand behind a bowing tree.

And Col was clutching for his legs.

Lew dived for a handful of grass and knifed the sand with the tent peg, still somehow in his fist. He could feel blood hammering in his ears. Col was groping near his knees, then near his feet and Lew kicked himself out of the gully. He glimpsed Col with his hands to his eyes, but he turned and kept climbing.

What's he doing here?

Lew felt the brittle brush scratch at his legs and arms, roots, grass catching at his feet. Already his muscles were hot, uncertain and tired, his lungs were pumping and Col, big Col, strong Col, very angry Col, was climbing again.

He'll catch you. Sure as hell he's going to catch you. Stop it. You can't panic now. Sure, he'll catch you if you keep going straight up. He's bigger.

Lew rammed the peg under his shorts and pushed sideways toward Mosstrooper, as Col lunged at him from too far below and too far back. Col fell heavily in the scrub.

That's a little better, see? But you saw Col get in the boat last night. And you saw the boat leave Border Island didn't you?

Something whirled past Lew's head. He looked back to see Col ten metres back, disappointed and empty-handed.

The hatchet. Look for it in the scrub ahead. See it?

Lew slowed a little and spread his hands as he pushed through the bushes.

No. Change direction, force him to lose the hatchet or risk losing you.

Lew started to climb again with the peak towering

over his head. Col hesitated a moment, switching his eyes from the receding Lew to the scrub that contained the hatchet. He shouted at Lew, then blundered after the hatchet. Lew wasn't sure whether he was relieved.

Lew was lashed by the brittle leaves of a bush and stumbled back a pace. He clutched at the bush as if he was fighting it, wrenched it aside and surged past, kicking a brief stream of little pebbles down the slope. He felt the air roaring in his throat.

No, don't panic now. But he's going to find that hatchet any second now and he's going to come running at you. Take it easy. Just keep moving away. But where, eh? Where he can't go faster than you, where big Col can't get near little Lew . . . Just where?

Col had stopped in a waist-high ridge of scrub and was searching through it with his arms. He was not looking up at Lew and for a moment he seemed to have forgotten the boy.

Of course. What happened was Theo dropped Col just round the point last night. So Col swam back into Cataran Bay and waited until stupid Lew got close enough to strike. Simple trap. Only worked on stupid kids.

For some reason that made Lew feel far better. Almost as if he was in control of things again.

Then Col plunged his right arm into the scrub and lifted the hatchet high in the air. He swung toward Lew, shouted and waved the hatchet at him. He began thrashing up the hill.

Maybe Mosstrooper. Maybe the bare granite ridges would slow Col, or Joe and Josie would get mad, or the wind would stop him. If you got out of sight for only a few seconds up there he'd never find you. All you have to do is get up there before he catches you.

Lew could look between his legs to see Col churning toward him, fast, violent and no more than twenty-five metres away. He was using the hatchet as a pick now, swinging it down through the scrub, catching it in the earth and pulling himself up behind it. Lew tried to move faster, but his ribs were pumping hopelessly, his stomach was hot and in pain, and his left leg was trembling every time he took a step. And any moment now Col would have another shot at him with the hatchet.

Col quickly cut Lew's lead to twenty metres as they hauled away from the bay, and Lew realized he was making a rough path for Col as he pushed through the scrub.

You can't stop him, you can't stop him, you can't . . . Less than fifteen metres now!

Lew was beginning to sob with every desperate breath he took.

Then the slope began to ease. Suddenly Lew was no longer clutching at rocks, brush, with his low swinging hands and he was taking longer, easier strides. He was reaching the saddle but Col was still battling the hill. Lew felt fresh wind on his face and looked back to see the distance between him and Col grow from fifteen metres to twenty, twenty-two, twenty-five, twenty-six!

He slanted his run to the beard of hoop pines below the face of Mosstrooper and for a moment air was sighing into his lungs. The pain retreated and his body began to relax.

Something clipped him on the right shoulder. He had time to frown before he saw the hatchet swing widely away from him and his shoulder jumped in pain. He looked back, saw Col standing with his legs apart and his right arm curved toward him.

He hit me!

Lew slapped his left hand to his injured shoulder, throwing his running rhythm into a short stagger which almost tumbled him sideways.

Don't be stupid.

He swung his hand back to his rhythm and shortened his pace as the hill steepened again. He glanced at his hand and noted with relief that it was not showing any blood. The pain in the shoulder was fading and he could move the arm without any trouble. He must have been hit by the hatchet's handle.

But Col was on the saddle now and gaining again. Lew scrambled across rock ridges and tangled grass as his fear gradually took over his legs and turned a ragged run into headlong flight. He was given a free moment when Col halted to pick up the hatchet again, but this time he did not use it at all. Lew reached the first pine no more than ten metres ahead of Col and he could not run much further.

But he could dodge. He lurched from one tree to the next, fully expecting the hatchet in his neck or a heavy hand on his shoulder, but Col's charge had become a clumsy stumble by the third tree. Lew turned his failing run into a wide-legged dance past trunks, bushes, vines and rocks. Tree ahead, sidestep, slap trunk, sidestep back, tree behind. And Col was slipping behind again, with his face dark with exhaustion.

We've got him. No, really, we've got him. Stay in the pines and he's never going to catch you. Wear him out. What d'you think he's doing to you? Never mind, we're winning.

A rock fall. A cliff. End of the pines.

Lew looked back over his shoulder and hesitated. Col caught his eye, was puzzled for an instant then lifted his eyes to the cliff. He grinned, an open leer revealing his yellow teeth, and lunged toward Lew.

Don't stop. Just don't stop.

Lew ran at the cliff and jumped without really aiming at anything. He clung to the granite like a fly on a wall, then felt himself slipping, beginning to fall back. But his right hand found a notch, a toe snagged a cleft and he had stopped. He looked up, grabbed a clump of spiky grass, kicked for a foothold and started climbing.

How close is he? No, don't look, just keep going.

He reached for a ledge, then both hands, then an elbow . . . and something clutched for his ankle.

Lew kicked out wildly with both feet, connected solidly with his left heel and rolled on to the ledge. He saw Col sliding back, shaking his head and skimming his huge hands over the granite. He was carrying the hatchet in his mouth.

Stopped him! Stopped—

But no. Col spread himself across the cliff and held on while pebbles bounced over his body. He took the hatchet from his mouth and swung it at the granite, hauling himself slowly up the cliff. He was staring at Lew, and he was saying, maybe shouting, a few angry words. Lew panted on the ledge and tried to read Col's lips.

'You *something* boy! I'm *something* going to lift your *something* little head off in a minute!' Col was shouting.

Have to move. Have to move, now!

But Lew's chest was heaving. He kept seeing patterns of coloured lights dancing before his eyes. He wanted to be sick. He couldn't run any more.

The hatchet crunched into the side of the ledge.

Lew recoiled as Col's other hand gripped the ledge a handspan from his shoulder. Col's face swayed up from the cliff, so close that Lew could feel the damp warmth of his breath. Col's eyes were wide with anger and pain, set in a face lined with grit, scratches and trickling sweat. One corner of his mouth was awash with saliva.

'Now clown boy, we're gonna see how *something* smart you *something* are!'

The hatchet lifted from the ledge. Lew scrabbled away.

And his right hand blundered over a loose rock, seized it and slammed it down on Col's other hand.

Col shouted, his damp breath blasting Lew's face, the hatchet swinging desperately back to the ledge as he fell away from the cliff. Two small birds erupted from some nearby scrub.

Lew dropped his rock limply beside him and watched his hand jumping about like a captured animal. He took some deep breaths before rolling back to the edge of the ledge.

Col was flat on his back at the foot of the cliff, his hatchet sticking in the bark of a pine. He was not moving.

God, I've killed him.

18

The Jump

Lew sagged back on the ledge and stared at the deep
blue ocean of the sky. Joe and Josie were again circling
a fleck of gold-rimmed cloud in their endless courting
dance and for a long moment he wished he could join
them. If he could release his grip on the earth and fall
effortlessly past the eagles to that tiny cloud island, the
one with the untouched golden beaches . . .

Come on. Maybe you can go down and help. Maybe
he's not dead yet. Okay, just give it a minute.

The panting died and the legs began to throb. Lew
wanted to stay motionless on the ledge for the rest of
the day, until the fear, the muscle ache, the pains and
the hopeless weight of exhaustion eased a little. But the
shouting in his head would not let him rest.

What happens if he's dead? What if there is nothing
in the box but a few tools and they only dropped them
because the boat was sinking? What, eh? What? You're
a thief, worse than Max, and a . . . they are going to
arrest you, have a long trial and throw you in jail
forever. Dad and Mum just wouldn't want to know.
They would, they would, and that would make it all
worse. Stop it, you've got to help. Now.

Lew pushed himself upright and looked over the
ledge for a way down.

Col was gone.

For one moment Lew was actually happy. His night-mare faded but it was almost immediately replaced by the return of the panic. He staggered to his feet and peered around him. There was no sign of Col below him and there was no sign of the hatchet either. Nothing but a small stone rolling to rest in the grass below and to his right.

He's coming up another way. You've got to keep on climbing.

Lew shook his head. He flexed his arms and felt the dead weight in them, but he started to climb again. Slower this time, and he felt every scrape of granite, every heave of a muscle. He didn't think he could run any more.

But this could work out. He can't see you now. That's all you wanted. Keep climbing, but climb to the right and he'll go for a place where you aren't. Climb under the eagle's nest and he'll wind up looking for you on the wrong side of the peak.

A pebble clipped Lew on the left ear and he looked up.

Col was standing on a rock above him, slapping his palm with the hatchet.

Lew turned desperately and stopped. He was stand-ing before a tumbling drop of more than fifteen metres, of ragged rock, corkscrew crevasses, crumbling ledges. He was as high as the tossing crowns of the hook pines, too high to scramble on that cliff face and hope to survive. If he climbed down Col would reach him before he could get out of reach. Col could grab him by the hair or just hit his hands with rocks the way he'd hit Col and watch him fall. He looked that mad.

Lew couldn't run, couldn't climb, couldn't do anything but wait.

Col eased himself over the rock and Lew saw blood trickling down behind his left ear.

'Got you, you *something* little *something*.' Col was breathing heavily and twisting his mouth as he spoke.

Lew looked at the black fury of Col's face, then looked away at the swaying treetops.

And jumped.

His throat tightened as the cliff slid away. His feet were swimming far above a shadowy patch of brush and grey rocks and he was beginning to drop. He forced his eyes away and up, up to the slowly bobbing pine top as it drifted toward his arms. He clutched at the tree, felt the pine needles in his fingers, brushing his face, and then it had passed. He was falling.

He began to shout.

His knee snagged a bending twig and swung him sideways. His right hand found the hard wood of the branch and he wrapped his body around it. He stopped with his fists full of needles, his left sandshoe half torn from his foot, swaying in the wind and staring back at Col with his mouth open.

Col stood on the cliff, shouting. He braced himself as if he was about to jump for Lew's tree, then shook his head, slapped the hatchet into his palm and turned away.

Lew watched Col climb out of sight in numb relief. He wheezed and lay limply on the branch, too weak to cheer. He felt a sharp pain high on his left leg and pulled the tent peg from his shorts, now bent and marked with blood.

It's all over. He's gone and there's no more running.

Lew drew his arm back to throw the peg away.

He hasn't gone at all! He's gone down to chop down your tree. Wake up, wake up.

Lew rammed the peg back into his shorts, jammed the sandshoe back on his foot and almost fell out of the tree. He dropped from branch to branch and hit the ground running. He glimpsed Col near the foot of the cliff as he bolted downhill through the forest.

Everything was wrong now. Col was between Lew and Mosstrooper, there were no more places to hide and Lew was just too tired to keep running. Lew burst from the trees, clutching at the air as if his arms could take over from his failing legs. He tried to reach concealing scrub on the northern arm of the bay, but Col raced on to the saddle, spotted him and began to run him down.

The water. It's got to be the water.

Ahead of him a smooth black rock sloped twenty metres into the water. If he could reach that he might escape. Just.

Lew reached the black rock ten seconds ahead of Col, squatted on his heels and started to skid. He felt the rubber under his feet ripple as the wind tugged at his shirt and he rushed toward the bay. He fought to keep his feet under him and under control, but the skid was turning into a fall. Lew jack-knifed his legs in a final effort to lift his toppling body clear of the rock and he hit the water like a bomb.

Immediately the network of scratches on his arms and legs began to sting, but his muscles stretched and relaxed. His face was washed clean and awake as he curved easily round a brain coral, and he didn't really want to return to the surface.

Just a breath and you stay deep and out of sight. Right?

But when he surfaced he saw Col staring at him from the top of the black rock.

Doesn't matter. He can't ride it. When he gets down to the water you'll be oceans away. You're a fish.

Col pulled the hatchet out of his belt.

Ah, go on, have a shot.

Col did not have a shot. Instead he ran straight down the black rock, hurling his feet over the rock, shouting, falling, slamming into the water no more than four metres from Lew.

Despairingly, Lew struck out for the bottom of the bay. He was near a skeletal staghorn forest when a hand gripped his ankle.

It would not let go.

19

Caught

Lew coughed for a long time. He seemed to be having trouble breathing. And he was being dragged somewhere, hoisted like a fish by one leg. Then left alone.

He opened his eyes slowly and saw his left foot dangling from a rock ledge. It was puzzling and it took him a few seconds to realize his foot was still connected to him and most of his body was lifted into the air. A strap or leather belt was round the ankle and the other end was held to the ledge by a tent peg driven through one of the buckle holes. His own tent peg.

He pulled at the peg, failed to move it and looked around him. He was now in the little bay and Col was sitting on his air tank, examining a knee. Col looked up, started to walk over to Lew, went back for the hatchet and slapped it on his hand as he approached Lew.

'Where is it?'

Lew worked his throat until he could feel his voice. 'What?'

Col drove the hatchet into the rock beside Lew's foot. 'I've *something something* from you, kid! Where is it?'

Lew was too tired, too sore to resist any more. 'Behind you,' he said.

'What are you *something* talking about?' Col nudged Lew hard with his foot.

Lew worked his tongue in his mouth and spoke very slowly. 'The box is behind you.'

'Eh? Behind me? Here? Where?'

'Behind that tree.' Lew pointed at the lush tree leaning out of the dense patch of jungle.

'Peewyn tut dwee? Talking *something* Eskimo now? Oh, behind that tree! Why didn't you say that?' Col turned and walked clumsily into the jungle. He stopped, hauled the box from a tangle of leaves and vines and shuffled back to the sand. He dumped the box two metres from Lew and sat on it.

'That easy,' he said and shook his head. 'Could *something* got it in an hour if Fat Theo'd used his head instead of his *something* to think with.' He looked up at Lew. 'Why?'

'Why what?'

'Don't get smart. Why did you hide it?'

'You knocked me over.'

'Jeez. That it?'

'And you were making a mess of my island.'

'Really? Your island?'

Lew looked away. It seemed stupid to him, too.

Col got to his feet and examined the lock. He seemed to be talking, but he had his back to Lew. Lew lifted his hips from the sand and tried to swing his foot free. The belt cut into his ankle and his foot swayed helplessly, but the tent peg moved.

Col hit the lock with the hatchet several times then shrugged and turned back to Lew. 'You didn't get it open, either. Know what's in it?'

Lew almost said something but shook his head. The

117

less he seemed to know the greater chance he would have of getting out of this.

'You didn't know what it is and you pinched it. And then you stay on the island? Kid, you are dumb.'

Lew nodded. He was hanging like a game fish being weighed. He'd lost Sunbird and everything. He had to agree.

'You deserve to have that boat sunk.'

Lew pressed his lips together. At least he was getting used to the rhythm of Col's lips now, reading almost everything he said. Maybe Col was understanding him better too. He glanced at the air tank and tried to change the subject.

'You came back underwater. That's why I didn't see you.'

Col smiled and sat on the box like a fisherman aglow with the tale of his catch. 'Jumped from Theo's boat just after we came out of the bay last night. Came here, dumped the tank and got to the beach in the early morning. Watched you for hours until you got close enough.'

'Then you caught me.'

'Almost didn't, eh?' Col almost smiled, then anger flashed across his face. 'You almost killed me on that cliff. You know that?'

'I was frightened.'

'You oughta be.'

Lew pressed his teeth on the tip of his tongue. 'Why don't you let me go? You've got the box now.'

'Oh, you're a real *something*, aren't you? Maybe Theo wants to talk to you.'

Lew felt a shudder in his breath. 'What for?'

'What for? Kidding, aren't you? Maybe Fat Theo

wants to sit on you. You get punished when you steal things. Don't you know that?'

We let Max go, never said a word to him, Lew thought. But he said: 'You go down deep with the tank?' Just keep him talking.

The anger faded from Col's face. 'Used to. Hundred feet down off the edge of the Reef.' He looked at the water and almost smiled. 'You got to wear a full suit and carry lights, but the fish! Man . . .' He almost closed his eyes.

'It must be great.'

Col looked at Lew as if he was surprised to find him there. 'All right.'

Lew nodded. He was losing Col now, and he didn't know what he could say to bring him back. Talk about the fire, no, about Sunbird, no, the box, anything . . . No, nothing to say at all.

The trapped boy and the weary youth stared at each other across the darkening beach for a long time.

'You've got to be a good hunter,' Col said suddenly.

'Eh?'

'Down there. With the tanks.' It was as if Col was pushing the chase, the box, Theo, even the old school fire, into the distant past. He could afford to relax now. 'Got me a groper once, big as me. True. I thought if I didn't get him, he'd get me. This is a good little bay. You catch much here?'

'I just swim around the coral here. But fishing's good round the point. Coral trout, coral cod. I used a line.'

'No spear? That's the way, y'know. A spear and a tank.'

'I want to learn to use a tank sometime. Not with a spear, just with a camera.'

119

'You have a go at it. Nothin' like it.'

'Maybe when I can afford it.'

Col chopped at a shell. 'Nice little boat, yours.'

Lew felt a faint stirring of anger, but he let it go. Now was not the time. 'Yeah.'

'Too bad.'

Lew blinked. Was that some sort of apology? 'Yeah.'

'How much did it cost?'

'Not much. Neighbour found it in a weed patch and didn't want it. Dad and me, we fixed up the hulls. Mum tried to sew the sails, but in the end she swapped two paintings for proper sails.'

'And she painted the sail.' Col's mouth hardened over the words.

'Yes.'

'Why?'

Lew did not understand. 'Why?'

'Why do your old man and your old woman do all that for you? Do they sail about on the boat? Do you pay them? Do you build houses for them? Eh?'

'I dunno.' Lew shrugged. He wanted the subject dropped.

'Do they do it because you're dumb?'

Lew started to say something then bit the words back. 'They like to do things, that's all. We get along.'

'Bull! They're all the same, all of them! You think your oldies are better than mine, that what you're saying?'

'No!' What's happening? It's all running wild.

Col stood up. 'My old man, he didn't like the idea of being a father, so he took a flit. I never saw him.' Col drove the hatchet absently against the box.

'Get it? He didn't like the percentage on sticking round for long enough for me to do things for him.

120

The old woman, Laura, stuck around a bit, until I wanted to do things my way. It got to be her boyfriend or me.'

Lew moved his mouth but stifled the words.

'The school fire? You are nothing, kid. Maybe I wanted to be caught. I lit the fire to teach Jackson a lesson and maybe to tell Laura I was still around. Okay, so she took the old man's hint and scarpered. Family trick.' Col hit the box several times.

'I would have given Aunt Emma the flit if she hadn't got in first. She took me in so everybody would know that she was a saint, not like her sister. But I wasn't helping her image much so she slammed her door and went back to singing in church.' A single blow and the lock on the box spun across the sand.

'And what about Fat Theo, eh? Fat Uncle Theo? What did he want from me? Just this.' Col snagged the lid of the box with the hatchet and levered it back.

Lew did not want to look but it was too late. With the lid off it did not matter whether he had seen inside or not, just that he had had the chance to see. He looked at the broad white sausages stacked closely in the box.

'He wanted me to dive for him. Smuggle things off the Reef. Know what this is?'

There was no use in pretending. 'Drugs.' He said flatly. 'Heroin.'

'You know all about it, eh?'

'It killed one of my friends.'

Col shrugged.

Lew couldn't leave it like that. Not with a shrug. 'Max Schulman. He was fourteen and he was going to be an astronomer. He found some funny mates and

121

they treated him to a shot in the arm, just to show him how great it was. He died six months later.'

Col drove the hatchet against the box. 'Who do you think you are, kid? Eh? I didn't stick your mate. Theo didn't stick your mate. We don't even know him.'

Lew remembered where he was and stayed silent.

'But it doesn't matter to you, does it, eh? You toffee-noses are all the same. Like Aunt Emma and so shocked at everything.'

Lew pressed his lips together.

'You really think your oldies are better than mine?' Col waved his hatchet at Lew. 'World's greatest sucker, you are.'

Lew was horrified now. Minutes ago he and Col had been almost friends and he could have hoped to be released before Theo arrived. Now Col was going mad and there was nothing he could do to stop it.

'Yeah, just think, deadhead. Maybe you embarrass them, you and the funny words and the clowning about. Maybe they want to say goodbye.'

'Come on, Col.'

'So they give you a super sailboat and let you sail by yourself all over the Whitsundays. Even as far as Border Island. Sooner or later a storm is going to get you.'

'That's the most ridiculous thing, ever.' But there was a sudden uncertainty in Lew's voice.

'Try and get permission to sail to Tahiti. You'll get it. They will be real happy to see you go.'

Lew shook his head very hard. 'It's stupid, it's—' And for a terrible moment he could remember Max alone with his shiny telescope and his parents leaving for yet another social affair. Max bribed and forgotten. Was he just another Max?

'It's not true!' Lew shouted.

Col cocked his head. 'Doesn't matter now,' he said, then walked past Lew to the twilight water.

A minute later Red Shark slid from the long shadow of the point.

20

Escape

Red Shark cruised into Cataran Bay as if it was finishing a long, lazy holiday. Theo was standing beside the wheel, leaning on the windscreen and looking intently at the main beach. Col waved his hand and his head jerked a little as if he was shouting. Theo looked sideways, grinned and swung toward the little bay. He shouted at Col but he was too far away and too much in shadow for Lew to watch his lips. Lew jammed his mouth shut to bottle up a rage of desperation.

What did he mean, 'Doesn't matter now'? Because of Theo? Why didn't Theo take an hour more to come back? Col was going to let you go after a while, wasn't he?

Lew pounded the sand with his fist, once.

Okay, he won't now. It's up to you.

Lew kept his eyes on the approaching speedboat but lifted his body as he kicked high, and again. He could feel his ankle throb and warm liquid was beginning to run on to his calf, but the peg had not moved.

Fat Theo stopped the boat's motor and threw out the anchor. The boat slewed gently on the rope, then bobbed slowly to rest in the shallow water.

'Was the *something something* easier to catch?' Theo

said as he jumped into the water. Lew could see his lips now, bloated and ugly.

Col said a few words and Theo looked surprised.

'Well you *something* get off the beer then. You're too fat.' Theo stopped in the shallows and looked hard at Lew. Not with anger or even dislike but more as a problem that has to be solved, a broken-down motor, a tree across the road, a sick cow. Somehow that was worse than open anger.

Col half-turned back to Lew. 'Well I caught him, anyway.'

Theo stormed past both Col and Lew to the box and he threw back the lid. 'What did he do?'

Col shrugged. 'Didn't. I opened it. To see if it was all right.'

'In front of him?' Jerking a thumb at Lew.

'He knew.'

'How'd *something something* he know?'

'Worked it out. He's not so dumb.'

Lew yanked at the peg. But I didn't say I knew! Why did you have to open the box. Why are you telling him that now?

Theo slammed the lid down and strode back to the boat. He almost walked over Lew but he did not spare him a glance.

Col was breathing heavily through his teeth.

Theo leaned into the boat and lifted a long piece of metal from behind the front seat. It took a few seconds for Lew to realize that the piece of metal was a shotgun.

They can't do this! They can't!

Lew felt he was screaming across the bay but he was only hissing softly. He arched his back to see Col's face but Col was moving away with his face set hard.

'Please . . .' Lew whispered. He raised his hand toward Col, as if to pull him back.

'What d'you want with that?' Col was saying.

Theo stopped, stared at Col and shook his head in disgust.

Say you're sorry, you'll never tell anyone, you'll say anything they want . . .

'Is it all there?' Theo said.

Lew felt moisture on his cheeks. He blinked but the men's faces swayed in a dark mist. He thrust his arm savagely across his eyes.

'—didn't count the bags,' said Col. 'Nobody opened the *something* before I did.'

'Well bloody check! All right?'

Col dragged the box away from Lew. He saw Lew's face and looked down and away, almost in shame.

What are you? Lew thought savagely. *Just a wimp, a bawling baby.*

At that moment Lew was so angry, so disgusted with himself he forgot to be afraid. He stared at the darkening sky and shouted silently at the moon. Somehow it felt better.

Col and Theo squatted next to a boulder eaten hollow by the tide and started counting the white sausages. Theo used the gun as a prop for a short while, then he leant the gun against the boulder, wheezed and sat in the sand.

Lew let his eyes move slowly from the sky to his throbbing ankle. The old brass buckle was cutting into his foot, the broad leather belt straining against the peg. He was straining so hard the buckle hole was being stretched from the peg. He could even see light between the peg, driven deeply into a cleft, and the rim of the hole.

Forget the peg, he thought. It's the belt. Move the hole.

Lew looked at Col and Theo, arguing angrily but almost with their backs to him. Then he saw the gun and he had to shake his head quickly to prevent the glance becoming a stare, with his thoughts trickling out on the sand.

Don't look and it doesn't exist. Oh, that's good, very good. Close your eyes and you're home in bed.

Lew jerked his eyes back to the peg. The peg was simply a straight piece of galvanised iron with a bend in the end, and the belt hole was no more than a thumb-length down the shaft. If he could just get the hole past the bend he would be free.

He wriggled quickly toward the rock wall until there was no room on the sand for his free leg. He watched the men while he lifted the free foot beside the trapped foot and moved closer to the wall. He was trying to climb the wall upside down. He lifted his buttocks and shouldered himself across the remaining span of sand, until he was almost standing on his head. Both his feet were higher than the peg and the belt was now dangling loosely between the peg and his ankle.

Theo slammed a white sausage down on the sand and shook his pointing finger under Col's nose. By the inflamed crimson on the back of Theo's neck Lew knew he was shouting.

Lew touched the buckle with a free toe and thought of loosening it a little to ease the pain of the trapped foot, but there was no time. He pushed his toes under the belt where it was pinned by the peg and tried to work it up. He felt it give, slide and even saw it move toward the bend.

Then it jammed. Lew heaved with his big toe, but

the toe bent and the belt tilted at the beginning of the bend. Lew yanked his trapped ankle away from the peg, but it snapped back at the end of the belt and a hot pain seared up his leg.

Theo pointed at his gun and shouted some more before swinging his arm back to point at Lew. And Col followed his finger to see for an instant Lew leaning upside down on the rock wall with his toes wrestling with the peg. His eyes shifted and caught Lew's face.

That's it, Lew thought. That's really it.

But Col turned his head back and kept on arguing with Theo as if he had seen nothing.

Lew bit the inside of his mouth, twisted his foot on the belt and kicked at the peg savagely. The peg bent without moving but the belt hole slid over the bend. Lew's trapped foot jarred against the rock, spraying the sand and Lew with grit and small pebbles.

Both Col and Theo looked up and Theo began to move.

But Lew was rolling down the beach, rolling on to his feet and running, limping toward the water with the belt coiling, snapping behind him.

21

The Net

Lew splashed into the bay, changing his running pace to a series of great strides. Then he remembered the gun and flung himself flat, sweeping his arms back even before he struck the water. He scudded over pale sand, grey pebbles and coral fragments and looked sideways to see a swarm of angry insects scar the surface of the sea. The insects lost their force in the first few centimetres below the surface and Lew realized that they were tiny fragments of lead riding comets' trails of air. A shot, and further ahead another shot.

C'mon, come on . . .

He could see the tawny mist of Red Shark's hull ahead and off to his left. He kicked himself down and forward, snatching at shells and weed to pull himself fast along the bottom. He looked back briefly to see the belt writhing like an eel attacking his ankle and further back the sudden white explosions of a man running in shallow water.

Col. And he is fast. Can he see me?

But Lew slid under the boat and pushed for the surface on the other side. His throat began to tremble, seeking air before he could breathe. He erupted from the water between the boat and the sunken boulders of the north shore and forced himself to gasp silently. He glimpsed Theo's head on the other side of the boat and ducked.

Too close. What to do? Forget everything and just swim flat out for the open sea. Past Theo and his gun, past Col? This is hopeless.

Theo was shouting, but he was looking away from him.

Slow down, clown. Please slow down.

Lew forced himself to take a long and shuddering breath. He moved closer to the boat and worked the strap from his leg in a few hurried seconds. His foot pulsed hotly but the strangled pain was gone. He dropped the belt, moved away and studied the water about him.

The sun was gone now. There were only tinted clouds and a pale moon in the sky, putting a softer silver sheen on the water that would hide its depth. That was good for a start. The boat was in the centre of the little bay, anchored a pace from the shore but carried out by a receding tide and a long loose rope.

Col and Theo were both looking for him on the south side of the boat. They could not see him now, but it was only a matter of time before they came round to his side of the boat. And he couldn't really move until they moved.

Lew moved to the stern of the boat to see where Col and Theo were now, kicking silently under the water, pushing himself along by placing his hands lightly on the hull.

Don't touch the boat! They'll see the movement.

Lew took his hands off the hull as if it had stung him, but he could not stop himself from drifting down to it. He banged his knee twice before he was able to scoop a metre of water between his body and the hull.

He ducked his head round the massive engine and saw Col swimming further out and shouting over his shoulder. He was close enough for Lew to understand what he was saying, but nobody seemed to have heard the banging.

'No, I can't see him!' Col was shouting. Lew found Col's lips moved slower when he was shouting, making the lips easier to read in the fading light.

For a few seconds Col looked as if he was listening, but Lew could not see Theo any more. He was picking up half a conversation.

'You wanna come out here yerself and look, hey?' Col waved a dripping hand over his head in a broad beckoning gesture.

'Yeah, I *something* well know he's got to breathe.' Col said a moment later. 'We'll get him.'

Col shrugged. 'I know! What about the *something* boat, eh? He could be hid—'

Lew duck-dived and stroked quickly away.

They are going to get me. They will. Shut up.

He looked back to see the boat jerk about and slip silently to the shore. Now he had to work out where he could break surface without being seen. As he swam toward the northern cliffs the coral bottom forced him closer to the surface and he knew that the white form of a swimmer in the shallows could be seen, even in moonlit water. A shadow ahead became a cleft between a large rock and the shoulder of a cliff, a cleft wide enough for Lew to kick into before he surfaced.

He looked up at an angular young heron and the heron blinked at him, possibly working out whether he could be eaten or whether he was dangerous. Lew forced a smile and the heron clicked its beak and walked away. Lew turned to the boat.

Theo placed the shotgun in the back of Red Shark, then climbed aboard with the anchor in his hand. He looked back for a moment at the box, shrugged a little and started the motor. He pointed at Col, then shouted. 'Come in here *something something*! You look along the sides. I'll watch from out there.' Red Shark moved toward Lew, then past to reach Col.

Lew looked desperately up the tumbled cliff to the straggled forest edge, at least five minutes of climbing in the open like an ant in a sugar bowl. The beach could be reached underwater but he would be seen long before he came up for air and it would take him another twenty seconds at least to reach the patch of jungle. And Col would find him in a few minutes if he stayed where he was. He was trapped, caught like a fish in a net.

C'mon, c'mon, there's got to be somewhere to go!

Theo suddenly looked over his shoulder at Lew. He groped for his gun, fired and shattered the heron on a near rock. Lew recoiled as if he had been hit. Theo shouted at Col and Col stroked past the boat, toward the flared body of the bird. Lew sucked in a lungful of air and clawed for the bottom again.

Underwater he could see Col's body thrashing to a spot on his left and the churning of Red Shark's motor receding behind him. He began to stroke away, toward the shallows of the beach, then he twisted in the water and aimed himself at Col's shadow on the bottom. He did not know why he had changed direction and it terrified him for a moment.

What are you doing? he screamed at himself. Get away! Get away . . .

Lew passed smoothly a metre and a half under Col's driving feet and pushed after the boat. Col just kept on going.

He didn't see, didn't see at all! Of course he didn't see. He had his eyes on that bird. The last place he'd look was under his feet. You knew that, didn't you?

Following the slowly descending bottom, Lew felt a cool current pushing down on him. He no longer had to fight to stay away from the surface and could concentrate on chasing the boat.

Okay, what do you think you're doing, eh? What d'you want with the boat? Of all the places to swim for . . .

Ahead and above Red Shark turned lazily.

Because it's the only place you can get a breath of air. Theo's going to be standing on the boat looking into the little bay. Col's going to be examining every rock, every weed on the sides of the bay. But nobody is going to be looking on the side of the boat that faces away from the little bay. Right? Maybe.

A large bubble escaped from the side of Lew's mouth.

If it stops. If it is close enough to reach.

Red Shark kept turning, turning away from the rapidly tiring boy. Lew felt his heart thundering in his chest and he imagined himself hammering a cork down his throat to keep the air in.

They've beaten me. They're just moving the boat out and out and waiting for me to come up. They know where I am.

The foam around the stern of Red Shark lessened to nothing as the boat turned again into the bay. It was stopping.

Just a little bit. Just get under the hull. Please.

Lew's stomach was beginning to heave. He couldn't

swim any more, just pulled himself tiredly along by fingerholds in the coral. His legs were drifting loosely and his body was lifting. The water was getting red.

Ah, c'mon . . .

He forced himself to look up, to see the hull ten metres ahead and far above his head.

Almost. Come on, you can do it!

He lifted from the coral, kicked and stroked as if he had just dived into the water and was chasing a coral trout. As if he was fresh, ready for anything and had lungs full of young sweet air.

On the fourth stroke air erupted from his mouth and he clenched his teeth to stop from gasping. He trailed in the water and allowed himself to be carried gently from the bottom.

He reached the surface an arm's length from the side of the boat, as silently as a jellyfish swimming, and took his first desperate breath with his hand shielding his mouth. Theo was standing on the bow with the anchor in his hands, his gun leaning on the windscreen, and his back to Lew.

Then Lew coughed, a spasm that shook his body from the pit of his stomach to his strained throat.

Theo looked around.

22

Fire

They just stared at each other; the heavy man tilting the boat slightly to starboard and the boy in the water, coughing, whooping air into his chest. The man blurred and his head swelled, stretched and distorted as a drop of water ran across Lew's right eyelid.

Then the boat rocked and Theo reached for the shotgun.

Lew's arms swept down as he kicked himself into the air, seeking height for a fast dive into deep water.

I can't swim, Lew thought hopelessly. Not any more.

He started to curl his body for the dive, then lunged sideways, throwing both arms over the boat's side. Theo seized the gun and picked it up as Lew hit the water, jerking the boat sideways and down. Theo swung the barrel down as the deck tilted violently. His face flickered from a gleam of satisfaction to open confusion as his feet danced desperately across the deck. He was already falling when his left foot snagged the anchor rope and the shotgun fired at a cloud as he crashed into the water.

Lew's mouth twitched into a smile, into a grin, into a silent yell of jubilation, as Theo fell. He began to release the boat.

No, don't stop!

He pushed himself up from the coaming, kicking as the boat rolled toward the other side and falling clumsily into the bottom of the boat. He could not stop gasping and his body wanted to give up and stop dead, but he could taste victory now. There was just enough strength left in his legs to hoist him onto his feet, to see Col standing on the shore, distant and defeated, and Theo, red and sodden, reaching for the bow.

He can still stop me . . .

Lew glanced over his shoulder and saw that the motor was still vibrating a little and therefore on. He leaned over the front seat and clicked the gear lever into drive. Theo lunged for the bow as Lew opened the throttle. He clutched for the anchor rope but was swatted aside as the boat surged forward.

Lew staggered back a step, caught at the back of the seat and hauled himself to the wheel as the boat flung itself at the north cliff. He jerked the wheel down and the cliff slid past the bow with a change of direction so savage it nearly threw Lew over the side. While Lew struggled for balance, Col, the beach and the southern cliffs raced past and the boat steadied on course for Theo's head and the open sea.

For an instant Lew thought of letting the boat run Theo down, but he moved the wheel quickly to clear him. He looked down at the man, his face dark with rage, and steered for Hook Island. He sighed and felt his body sag.

Don't have to go far, really. Get Sarge on the radio, and—

The motor shuddered, roared and was strangled. The boat flowed on for two seconds then jerked to a halt as if it had hit a sandbar.

Lew looked back. The boat was drifting back and suddenly Theo was smiling. He started to paddle after the boat as Col took a racing dive from a rock.

What's happened? It can't stop me now!

He revved the motor and oily blue smoke rose from the stern. He revved again and the motor coughed and cut out. He clambered over the seat back, touched the motor, felt a searing pain and jumped back with four burned fingers. But he had seen enough. The anchor line was now a heavy ball of rope and chain tangled around the propeller. The stern of the boat was tethered to the anchor at the bottom and muzzled like a savage dog.

And Theo was eight metres away, with Col closing fast.

A knife. Please, a knife to cut the rope.

Lew searched the bottom of the boat and tumbled back into the front seats to find only rags, lengths of wire, cigarettes, Theo's lighter, a boat hook and a handful of shells for Theo's shotgun. Nothing and too late.

Theo reached the boat and began to haul himself aboard.

Lew snatched at the boathook and hit Theo on the head with it. Theo recoiled, shook his head and swam back. He started to shout, then closed his mouth and smiled.

'You are gonna go, kid,' he said slowly and precisely. He did not make any other attempt to board the boat. He was waiting for Col.

Lew trailed the boathook in the water and hung his head. There was nothing more he could do, was there? He was finally beaten.

He opened his left hand and blinked at the cigarette lighter.

Well, there was a thing he could do. Not much, but it would do.

He dropped to his knee beside the large fuel container for the motor and unscrewed the cap. Theo realized what was happening and swam in hurriedly.

Lew snatched a rag from the bottom of the boat and began ramming it into the petrol tank.

'You stupid kid!' Theo slammed his arm down on the boat's side, tilting the boat beneath Lew's feet.

Lew looked back at the tank, pushing at the rag, raising tiny puffs of dust between his forefinger and thumb. Half-way in, three-quarters . . . Stop. Pull back until the petrol stings the skin and it spreads a dark stain on the floorboards.

Theo rose in a great surge of boiling water, his arms rigid and quivering on the edge of the boat, his fat toe writhing for a hold. Lew moved to the other side and clicked the lighter. Clicked it many times.

'What are . . .' Theo panted and swept his clutching right hand to within a handspan of Lew's face. He was now balancing on one arm with the boat turning, tilting toward him.

The lighter flared into life. A long finger of flame shot from between Lew's finger and thumb. He almost grinned.

'. . . you doing?' Theo pulled his hand back as he stared at the flame.

'Go!' Lew waved the flaming lighter over the spreading petrol. Go, get off the boat or I will destroy it.

'Don't be silly, boy . . .'

'Go, now!' Lew jerked the lighter at Theo. And fumbled. He felt the greasy metal of the lighter slither in his palm, grabbed at it and saw it pop free. For one instant the lighter was in the air, the cap jammed and the long flame curving back, then it began to fall.

'Heeh!' Theo threw himself from the boat.

Lew made a last despairing attempt to catch the lighter but the boat leapt under his feet and he clutched at the flame. The lighter hit the petrol-soaked rag and he rolled into the water a second before the explosion.

Underwater Lew was pounded in the back, winded and tumbled into the deep. Streams of tiny bubbles sped past him on the way down, then a dying fish curled and uncurled under him before working its way up past his shoulder.

He supposed he had better go up to the surface too and breathe, but there didn't seem to be any urgency this time. He swam a few slow strokes then allowed himself to be carried limply to the surface. He was surprised when he gasped loudly in the air.

Red Shark was ablaze, a floating bonfire so intense the boat seemed to have disappeared behind a curtain of flame on the water. Shadows and shoals of bright streamers rippled up the slopes of Mosstrooper, catching flashing jewels in the rocks. Above the fire the air shimmered, twisted then erupted into a billowing column of thick smoke that blotted out the moon as heavy black drops fell constantly into the water. One of the drops hit Lew's shoulder, splattering, burning and driving him to swim to the rocks.

He hauled himself from the water as the black shower eased, turned clumsily and sat back. His ribs were flaring, his mouth yawed wide and he felt dizzy. His shoulder burned; his ankle felt the cut of the belt as if it was still there. All over his legs, arms and belly cuts and scratches were stinging with the salt, and his right leg would not stop trembling.

He saw Theo crawl on to a rock ten metres away, his face smeared with blood, and Col now swimming straight at him. They were both staring at him, too angry to speak but with their eyes drawn back in slits. Lew tried to stand, tried to get back into the water, but his muscles would not obey him and he fell back.

Theo looked back at the slowly sinking wreck of his boat and jerked himself to his feet. He stumbled forward, wheezing and with his hands curled into claws. Col took two quick strokes and rose from the water with a seamed rock in his hands.

And Lew lay back on his rock and gasped. There was nothing at all he could do.

Col hefted his rock, then he frowned and lifted his eyes from Lew. He stood like that for a few seconds then hurled his rock in fury—not at Lew, but at the low cliff near Theo. Theo slumped in mid-step, sighed and sat on a rock, his anger trickling away from him.

'You are *something* lucky,' Col said tiredly, and turned away.

Lew looked behind him at the western point of Cataran Bay and the open sea.

And at the bright orange bulk of the police boat, coming in with the battered carcass of Sunbird humped behind its cabin.

23

Beached

Lew stopped in the hall of his house and rested a finger on Mum's small jade figurine, a shimmering Chinese princess smiling at an old secret. He guessed he would always remember Max when he saw the princess. There was no avoiding that, but he would try to remember the better Max that had gone before. Not the Max who had run from home to escape medical treatment near the end, not the twitchy boy that needed the needle like he needed air and would steal from his best friends to pay for it. No, he was gone, now.

Lew would remember only the bright-eyed kid who somersaulted round his telescope late at night yelling that he had found Jupiter, the red giant, and quick, come and look! He could at least do that.

Lew turned from the figurine and walked into the back yard, to Dad working fibreglass into one of the holes in the port hull of Sunbird. Mum was staring at Sunbird and looked up at Lew with her lips pursed, as if *he* had attacked the boat with an axe.

Dad straightened up with a smile. 'It's not too bad,' he said. 'Bit of work, but we can fix it.'

Lew thought about Col in the cove at Border Island and could almost see a dark shadow on Dad's face.

'Ah, cheer up. We can make it as good as it ever was. Better. You can be sailing to your island any time . . . anything wrong?'

Lew snapped up his head. Why don't you ask him if you can sail to Tahiti?

'No!' Mum said.

'What's up, love?'

'He's not sailing to Border Island, or any island, and that's final.' Mum's eyes were hard. 'How can you forget that radio message from Sergeant Austin?'

'It's over now, love. Over for a week.'

'I feel it now! Lew's boat found abandoned and awash off north Hook Island. My God, I might be a biddy but after that night I want him right here!'

'Come on, it wasn't that long a wait. Just until Austin zipped from Hook Island to Border—'

'And found him about to be killed by two drug runners. I still want to claw the eyes from both the Starkeys. I hope they never get out of prison.'

Dad smiled. 'Your mother was a little upset that night.'

'You weren't? Lew, your clever father was just about ready to look for you beyond Hook Island in a rowboat. With a torch.'

Dad coughed. 'I think your mother's right. We'll fix your boat, but for a while, just sail it off Airlie Beach, where we can watch you. Okay?'

'Okay.'

Dad looked surprised, but Lew had thought about his island almost all the time since he got home. When he pictured the magnificence of the Throne he remembered the sad ghost of Max, almost telling him the secret of the box. When he pictured the saddle, that was where he'd stood while Sunbird was butchered;

142

the beach was where he had begun to run for his life; the grim face of Mosstrooper was where he had almost killed a man. If he swam in Cataran Bay he would see the charred wreckage of the boat he had sent down to crush a forest of delicate coral staghorns. No he wouldn't want to go back to Border Island for a while. He would miss the eagles, but the island was no longer his.

And anyway, for some reason he wanted to stay around the place a bit. Watch Mum paint, go fishing with Dad. Funny.

'Col Starkey,' said Lew abruptly. 'Will they keep him in jail a long while?'

'You worried about him?'

'No. Not any more.'

'That's right. He'll be in there a few years for the drug running and for what he nearly did to you. Want to see him punished real bad?'

'No. He didn't really do much.'

'You're beginning to sound like you two were the best of friends.'

'Feeling sorry for him.'

Lew thought of Col in prison, alone. His dad, a continent away, would never hear about him; his mum would hear about him but would probably ignore him; Aunt Emma would hear, but she'd only visit him to tell him how useless he was; and Uncle Theo, if he ever wanted to visit Col they'd never let him. He'd be in a tougher prison for longer.

'You're a mad kid, y'know that?' said Lew's dad.

Lew grinned at his 'oldies'. 'But Col was right.'

'What?'

'Said I was something lucky.'

'I give up,' said Dad. 'You tackle him, love. I can't understand a word the boy says.'

143